WILLIAM'S CROWDED HOURS

"IF I'D HAD ANYONE BUT YOU FOR A BROTHER," SAID
ROBERT, "I MIGHT HAVE WON HER BY NOW."

(See page 233.)

WILLIAM'S CROWDED HOURS

BY

RICHMAL CROMPTON

ILLUSTRATED BY
THOMAS HENRY

LONDON
GEORGE NEWNES LIMITED
TOWER HOUSE, SOUTHAMPTON STREET
STRAND, W.C. 2

First Published	.	.	.	*1931*
Fifteenth Impression	.	.	*1948*
Sixteenth Impression	.	.	*1951*
Seventeenth Impression	.	.	*1954*

Printed in Great Britain by
Wyman & Sons, Ltd., London, Fakenham and Reading

CONTENTS

CHAPTER I

WILLIAM AND THE SPY

THE members of William's family were having their annual holiday by the sea. They were staying in the boarding-house in which they generally stayed. The Browns chose it because it did not object to William. It was not enough for the Browns to go to a boarding-house that did not object to children. It had to be one that did not object to William. This boarding-house was of a philosophical, if pessimistic nature and took it as in the natural course of things that William's crabs should make their home in the hatstand drawer, that 'pieces' from William's collection of seaweed should make the hall into a sort of skating rink, and that William himself should leave a trail of sand and shells and jelly-fish wherever he went. William, however, was enjoying this holiday less than the other members of his family. Though indulging to the full in the delights of the seaside, he considered them to be greatly overrated. Paddling was a pastime whose possibilities were soon exhausted. He could make it exciting by pretending that he was wading into the sea to rescue shipwrecked sailors or pull to shore a boat of smuggled goods, but he always entered too wholeheartedly into these games and arrived home soaked to the neck. Paddling was generally forbidden by his mother after the third day at the seaside, because, as she said, he only had three suits, and, when he got them all soaked in one day, there was nothing to fall back on.

It happened to be too cold for swimming, for which Mrs. Brown was thankful, because last year the other swimmers had grown so tired of rescuing William that they had threatened to let him drown the next time he got into difficulties.

When paddling was forbidden, William took to exploring the rocks with results even more disastrous than those of paddling, for there were pools of water among the rocks into which he was always falling, as well as jagged surfaces down which he was always sliding. His mother's attitude to this annoyed William almost beyond expression.

"How d'you think I'm ever goin' to be able to have any sort of adventure when I grow up if I don't try'n' get a bit of practice now?" he protested passionately. "How d'you think Hereward the Wake 'd ever have been a hero if his mother had gone on at him like what you do at me whenever he got his suits wet?"

'I don't know how many suits Hereward the Wake had," said Mrs. Brown firmly, "but, if he only had three and had soaked two and torn the third, I don't see what his mother could have done but make him stay indoors till one of them was fit to wear."

And so it came about that William was sitting in the drawing-room of the boarding-house in his dressing-gown, while two of his suits dried before the kitchen fire, and the third was at the tailor's having a new seat put in.

William had never patronised the drawing-room before, and the novelty of the situation rather intrigued him. There was an old lady in an arm-chair by the fire who had already requisitioned him to hold her wool for her to wind. William disliked holding wool for people to wind, and with a skill born of long practice had managed to get it into such a tangle without apparently moving his hands at all, that the old lady had given up the whole thing in despair and gone to sleep. On the other side of the fire sat another lady, tall and thin and middle-aged, engaged upon a piece of crochet work and wearing a pair of pince-nez balanced on the very end of her nose. Between her and the sleeping old lady was a circle of other ladies, all middle-aged and thin and spectacled and engaged upon needlework of some sort. William, clad in his dressing-gown and forming part of the circle though completely ignored by it, gazed around at them with deep interest. He had had no idea that all these women were different. He always came in to meals when everyone else had finished, and, meeting these visitors occasionally in the passages, he had thought that there was only one of them.

Now he looked round at them with the thrill of the discoverer. . . . One, two, three, four, five, six, and so much alike that he had thought they were all the same.

The one by the fire was talking. Her name was Miss Smithers. She had lived an utterly uneventful life and had never had anything to talk about till the war came. She hadn't yet realised that most people had stopped talking about the war.

"Of course," she was saying, "the country had been *full* of their spies for *years* before the war began. They'd come over as tourists or students or even professors—and they'd pass as Englishmen *anywhere*, you know, they're such clever linguists—and they'd each take a tiny bit of the coast line and *study* it till they knew every *inch* of it. *Riddled* with spies, the country was. And what they've done once they can do again. . . . We're never on our guard."

The others, who had heard it all before, were not taking any notice, but William was sitting forward, eyes and mouth wide open, drinking in her words. The war had been over before William was born, and William's immediate circle was one that lived in the present. He had never heard anything like this before. . . . Most thrilling of all was the "And what they've done once they can do again."

He was just going to demand further details, when his mother opened the door to tell him that one of his suits was dry now and he could go and put it on. He followed her into the hall. There stood an elderly man with a short, white beard talking to the proprietress. He held a suit-case in his hand and had evidently just arrived. He was saying, "I'm a geologist, you know. I've come here to study this part of the coast."

And then, of course, William knew beyond a shadow of doubt that he was a German spy who had come over to prepare for the next war.

* * * * *

"What's a geologist?" William asked his mother as he struggled into his suit that, though dry, was still strongly perfumed with seaweed.

"A man who studies rocks," said his mother.

William uttered an ironic laugh.

"That's a *jolly* easy way to do it," he said.

"What are you talking about?" said his mother, who was looking doubtfully at his suit and wondering whether it had been as much too small for him as that before its immersion in sea water.

But William merely repeated his ironic laugh.

The next morning William set off to a withdrawn spot among the rocks that had already served him as a Red Indian camp and a pirate's ship, and there he held a meeting of the secret service men under his command. They all saluted him respectfully as he entered—a magnificent figure in a blazing uniform with jingling spurs. He informed them curtly of the danger (there were, of course, innumerable Germans studying each a mile or so of the coast) and warned them that the work on which he was sending them would probably mean death (he was a ruthless man with no compunction at all in sending his men to their death, but he went to his own so bravely and so continually that they could not resent it). Then, after ordering them each to dog one spy and report to him daily, he gave them the secret code and password, and explained the complicated system of signals by which they were to communicate with each other and with him. He warned them to expect no mercy from him if they failed. That, of course, was part of his ruthlessness, for which nevertheless they all adored him. An ordinary passer-by would have seen nothing of this. He would merely have seen a small boy in a suit that had obviously suffered as the result of frequent immersion in sea water, playing by himself in a hollow among the rocks. Ordinary passers-by, of course, never see things as they really are.

At the end of the meeting William changed his rôle to that of one of the secret service men (the best and most promising of them, whose courage had already been tried in many a desperate adventure) and, saluting the magnificent figure in the resplendent uniform, emerged from the rocks after making elaborate precautions to escape detection. With his collar turned up, and his head sunk into it so deeply that nothing of his face could be seen but the tip of his nose, he set off in order to shadow his victim.

* * * * *

Professor Sommerton was not at all surprised to find himself dogged throughout the morning by a small boy. He had learnt that, wherever one was and whatever one was doing, small boys always hung about to watch and if possible annoy one. This small boy was rather odd in his behaviour (for instance one could see nothing at all of his face, as he kept his cap pulled down and his coat collar turned up, and he followed one in an extra-ordinary fashion, sidling along by the rocks), but then the professor considered all small boys to be odd in their behaviour, differing only in degrees of oddness, and he disliked them all uniformly. This boy, however, really began to get on his nerves as the morning wore on, and he returned to the boarding-house earlier than he had meant to, only to discover to his annoyance that he had lost the sheet of paper on which he had been making his shorthand notes. At that very moment William was entering the hollow in the rocks still with elaborate precaution of secrecy—gazing round on all sides to see that the coast was clear and then pulling up his coat collar so high that one of the sleeves gave audibly beneath the strain—and handing the sheet of paper to the chief in the magnificent uniform.

"Here's his code what I've got at deadly peril," he was saying. "If he'd seen me he'd've killed me. He'd gotter special pistol in his pocket made to look like a fountain-pen an' I bet if he'd've seen me I'd've been dead by now."

The magnificent chief read the paper with many a low whistle and exclamation of "Gosh!"

He said that none of the others had done so well and promoted William to be second-in-command.

"When you hear of me bein' killed by crim'nals," he said, "what I'm likely to be any minute, you jus' carry on here. Seems to me you're the bravest man I've ever come across—next to me, of course."

William went home well satisfied by his morning's work. The professor was less satisfied.

"Most tiresome," William heard him say at lunch. "I lost the paper on which were the results of my whole morning's work."

He met William's eye—a completely blank eye—and sighed. He did not connect William with the boy who had haunted him all the morning, but he felt vaguely that the world would be a more peaceful place if there were no small boys in it.

After lunch he went out to the rocks and set to work again. He had a tape measure and a little hammer, and he worked hard, stopping every now and then to make notes or to add to the contours of a rough map that he was making. Again the boy was there, peering at him between the buttonholes of his coat (which was pulled up till the collar was on a level with the top of his head, and which now showed a large rent round the sleeve), crawling after him on hands and knees, watching him from inadequate hiding-places among the rocks, sidling around him in a way that distracted the professor indescribably. And then when he reached the boarding-house he found that he had lost the map that contained the results of his afternoon's work.

William was seated in the hollow among the rocks. He had grown tired of the magnificent chief and had had him killed by criminals. He was holding a meeting of the other secret service men and telling them that the chief had been killed by criminals and that he was now in sole charge. He told them that he had got both the code and the map from his spy, and asked how they had been getting on. They had, of course, no results at all to show him, and he was very stern with them.

*   *   *   *   *

The professor set out the next morning with a firm determination to send that boy about his business— by force if needs be. The whole situation was getting on his nerves. He was sure that he would never have lost those papers if it hadn't been for that boy's distracting his attention by his antics.

He went a longer way down the coast than usual. William followed him as before, slipping from rock to rock. William was blissfully unaware that his quarry had even caught a glimpse of him. He imagined that, thanks to his methods of secrecy, he had been completely invisible to him all the time. It was therefore an unpleasant surprise when, as he was engaged on watching his victim on hands and knees from the shadow of a rock, his victim turned on him savagely and said:

"I've had enough of your monkey tricks, my boy. Clear off and be quick about it."

William rose to his feet with dignity. He thought it best now to reveal himself in his true colours.

"Yes," he said, "I bet you'd like me to clear off. I bet you don't know who I am?"

"Who are you then?" said the professor irritably.

"I know all about *you*," said William darkly. "I know what you're doin' an' where you've come from an' I've got your code so it's no use tryin' to send any secret messages, an' my men are all surroundin' you so it's no use trying to escape an'——"

"Clear off," roared the professor angrily, "and don't give me any more of your impudence."

"CLEAR OFF," ROARED THE PROFESSOR ANGRILY, "AND DON'T GIVE ME ANY MORE OF YOUR IMPUDENCE."

William was slightly nonplussed by this attitude. The man should have been cowering at his feet and begging for mercy by now. Suddenly the professor made a threatening gesture with his hammer and roared again, "Clear off." William lost no time in clearing off. He told himself when he reached the promenade that his life was of too great service to his country for him to risk it unduly. He stood on the promenade wondering what to do. His afternoon's dogging of his victim had not improved his never-very-spruce appearance. His grown-up sister passed him at that moment with an immaculate youth in tow. She passed him with bated breath and eyes staring glassily in front of her, in fear lest William should see and recognise her. William was too much engrossed in his problem to have eyes for Ethel and her escort. In any case he cherished a healthy contempt for Ethel's idea of pleasure. He went down to the beach and threw stones idly into the sea while he pondered what was best to do. Some people who were swimming came out of the sea to remonstrate, and William moved away with dignity to an unattended boat, in which he sat trying to look as if it belonged to him and continuing his mental wrestling with his problems.

He might, of course, go to the hollow in the rocks to report, but he was growing tired of the hollow in the rocks. He had that morning, as he dressed, sent a messenger to dismiss all the other secret service workers so that he needn't be bothered with them any more. There was no doubt at all, however, that the man was a spy and that it was his duty to bring him to justice. He sat up and looked about him. Along the promenade a policeman was coming with slow and measured tread. That was the best thing to do, of course. Tell a policeman about it and leave him to catch the spy and put him in prison. William realised suddenly that there were a lot of interesting things he wanted to do, and that it would be quite a relief to get rid of his spy by handing him over to justice.   He made his way up to the promenade and followed the policeman, dodging in and out of people's legs till he caught him up.

"Please!" he said breathlessly.

The policeman turned.   He had a fierce moustache, and eyebrows that were fiercer still.   William looked at him and decided to find one who looked a little more sympathetic before he told his tale.

"Well," the policeman had snapped, "what d'you want?"

"What's the time please?" said William meekly.

"Use your eyes," said the policeman, pointing to the Tower Clock a few yards away.

Then he continued his walk with slow dignity.

William stood staring after him sternly.   In imagination he had reassumed the character of the late magnificent chief in order to deal with the policeman, and the policeman was pleading abjectly to him for his life.   William treated the policeman to some of his famous ruthlessness, before he finally pardoned him. His self-respect restored by this proceeding, William went on down the promenade.   He met Ethel again with the immaculate youth and pulled his most hideous grimace at them.   The immaculate youth drew himself up, outraged and affronted, and Ethel passed on with an angry, glassy stare.   William knew that Ethel would disclaim all knowledge of him and then would live in terror of the immaculate youth's discovering that he was her brother.   Between William and Ethel there existed a state of continual warfare.   What Ethel gained in the authority that accrued to her added years she lost by that respect for appearances that frequently laid her at William's mercy, and so they were about equally matched as adversaries. Up-lifted in spirit by this encounter, William turned off the promenade into one of the crowded streets that led to it. At the end of it he saw a policeman regulating the traffic. He was the policeman of one's dreams. He radiated kindness and sympathy in every glance and movement. William felt that this was the one police-man of all the policemen in the world in whom he must confide his story of the spy. Narrowly escaping death beneath the wheels of several cars, he crossed the road to the middle, where the policeman, waving on one line of traffic and holding up another, looked down at him and said, "You'll cross the street like that once too often one day, my lad."

William, however, had not come to discuss his methods of crossing streets.

"There's a spy down on the beach," he said breath-lessly, "he's measuring it out an' making a map ready for the next war. You'll catch him if you're quick."

The policeman looked down at him, still kindly and amused.

"Now, my lad, don't try any of your funny work on me, because I haven't time for it."

Whereupon he held up the traffic for William to continue his passage of the street. Disconcerted, William continued it. He stood doubtfully on the further pavement, wondering what to do next. He was convinced that, if this policeman wouldn't believe him, none would. And the responsibility of bringing his spy to justice had begun to weigh heavily upon his spirit. He wandered slowly back to the shore, climbed into the unattended boat again and sat there thinking. As he scowled out over the sea, his head between his hands, he uttered his famous sardonic laugh. He knew why they wouldn't believe him. They thought of him as a child. They'd no idea what he really was. If he could get a grown-up to see what the spy was doing, it would be all right. The policeman would believe a grown-up. They always believed grown-ups.

"Now then!" said a voice behind him, "nip out o' this an' look sharp."

William turned. The boatman to whom the boat belonged had come upon him unawares. He was a large man with a red face and a twinkle in his eye that belied his fierce voice.

"'Less of course," he went on with obvious sarcasm, "you're wantin' a row an' willin' to pay for it."

And then suddenly the idea came to William. Here was his witness, the grown-up who should catch the spy red-handed and give him over to the police. The spy would be keeping a look out upon the land, of course, but he worked with his back to the sea and he wouldn't be prepared for any one coming upon him from that quarter.

"If you found a spy spyin'," said William, "would you give him up to the police?"

"You bet," said the man, winking at the breaker for want of anything else to wink at. "Why, I've caught dozens of 'em in my time."

William felt in his pocket. There reposed in it a sixpence that his father had given him that morning.

"Yes, I'll have a sail," said William, "a sixpenny one, please."

"How far d'you think you'll get for sixpence?" said the man scornfully.

"I'll get as far as I want to get," said William, "an' I'll jolly well show you somethin' that you din't know was there."

There seemed to be no other prospective customer in sight, so the man good-naturedly pushed off his boat and jumped into it. William watched him with envy. He had often wanted to do that. Once he got this spy business over, he'd see if he could learn how to do

THEY ROUNDED THE POINT, AND THERE, CLINGING TO THE ROCKS, WAS THE PROFESSOR.

it. It probably wasn't as hard as it looked. There were lots of unattended boats along the beach that he could practise on.

"Well, where d'you want to go?" said the man.

"Keep close along the coast," said William, "it's jus' round that big rock—the bit you can't see from here."

The boatman, thinking rightly that William would be a credulous audience, began to tell him about the sea serpents he had seen in his youth, but William's response was half-hearted. He was living for the

"MY RESCUER!" HE CRIED. "MY NOBLE RESCUER."

moment when they should steal upon the spy from behind, and catch him engaged upon his nefarious work. Then there was that next and just-as-thrilling moment to think about, when the burly boatman should hand him over to the police, and William should tell how he had shadowed him and finally caught him.

"Round this 'ere point, did you say?" asked the boatman.

"Yes."

"You can't land there, you know, now," said the boatman, "it's high tide."

At that moment they rounded the point, and there, clinging in terror to the rocks, waist high in water, was the professor. As soon as he saw William and the boat, he gave a shout of joy.

"My rescuer!" he cried, "my noble rescuer!"

*   *   *   *   *

It was the next day. William was walking along the sea coast to the line of rocks beyond the beach. He had spent last evening in a blaze of glory. The professor had told the story eloquently to everyone in the boarding-house. "This boy was playing about near me while I was working, and I sent him away because it worries me to have boys playing about near me when I'm working. He went away and later on he noticed that I had not returned, and, knowing that it would be high tide and that the rocks where I had been working would be covered (a fact that I had foolishly omitted to ascertain), the brave boy quietly hired a boat to come to my rescue. He saved my life. . . ."

William, who was beginning to have a dim suspicion that the professor was not a spy after all, saw no reason to contradict the story. If the notoriety of having captured a dangerous spy were denied one, that of having rescued a celebrated professor of geology was better than nothing. He received the plaudits of the boarding-house with modest nonchalance.

"Oh, that's nothin'," he said, "I'd do that for any-one any time. Savin' a person from drownin's nothin'."

To mark his gratitude the professor presented

William with a ticket to a lecture that he was giving in the town that evening on Geology. William went to it, and it confirmed his suspicions that the professor was not a spy, because he was sure that no spy could make quite as dull a speech as the professor made. Further to mark his gratitude, the professor gave William's mother five pounds to add to William's post office savings account. William thanked him perfunctorily. William looked upon his post office savings account as a deliberate scheme of his parents to divert from him any money that might come his way.

But it was now the next morning, and everyone, William included, was beginning to forget that he had saved the professor from a watery grave the day before. William was tired of being a secret service agent. He had decided to be a spy. He was an English spy in a foreign land. He had a piece of tape, stolen from his mother's work bag, and a piece of stick to represent a hammer. With them he measured and tapped the rocks, stopping occasionally to scrawl hieroglyphics on a piece of paper. Sometimes imaginary natives of the place would pass, and William would slip the tokens of his trade into his pocket and talk to them volubly in their own language, explaining that he was a professor of geology. He brought all the foreign words he knew into these conversations. "*Hic, hæc, hoc,*" he would say, "*Je suis, tu es, il est, mensa mensa mensam, la plume de ma tante, dominus domine dominum*——"

After a short conversation of this sort the imagined foreigners would pass on their way, completely deceived, and William would return to his tapping and measuring.

He was perfectly happy. . . .

CHAPTER II

THE PLAN THAT FAILED

WILLIAM sauntered slowly down the road towards school. His person was freely decorated with bandages that were the results of a skirmish between William and a new geyser that his family had lately had installed. The man who installed it had said in answer to Mrs. Brown's enquiries: "No, Madam, it's a new model and it can't possibly explode. I defy anyone," he had added "to make this geyser explode." It was a very foolish thing to say in the hearing of William, but then, of course, he did not know William. William had accepted the statement as a challenge, and had worked hard and conscientiously on the new geyser till he made it explode. When finally they picked him up from the débris (after ascertaining that the house still stood) his first remark had been a triumphant: "There! And he said it couldn't explode!"

The attitude of his family annoyed him.

"Well," he said, "someone'd got to find out if he was telling the truth, hadn't they? You can't have a man goin' about tellin' stories like that all over the place, can you? Well, he *was* tellin' stories. It *did* explode, didn't it?"

William considered himself an investigator in the cause of Truth and Science, and, when one considers oneself an investigator in the cause of Truth and

Science, it is annoying to be treated by one's immediate circle as a criminal. They considered, however, that his injuries were sufficient punishment, and this attitude further increased William's annoyance.

"I like that!" he said indignantly. "Who ought to be punished—the one that tells stories or the one that finds out about them being stories? *He* ought to've been blown up by rights. I'm glad it was me and not him, though, because I've always wanted to know what it felt like to be blown up."

"Don't talk so much, William," said his mother patiently, "and try to go to sleep."

This advice stimulated William to aggressive wakefulness for some minutes, but at last, still muttering indignantly to himself, he fell asleep unawares.

He found the days of enforced rest tedious in the extreme. The doctor's nauseous medicine and caustic comments enraged him, and even his mother's patient ministrations seemed an insult to him.

"Don't you think he might get up now?" he overheard his mother say to the doctor outside his bedroom.

"He could, of course," said the doctor, "but I thought that an extra day or two might complete nature's punishment."

"Oh, please let him get up," said Mrs. Brown. "It's far more a punishment for me than for him."

So William got up and at once his spirits brightened. The sight of his face swathed in bandages pleased him immensely. He swaggered about the garden, recounting to imaginary audiences the heroic struggles with lions, tigers or leopards in which he had received his wounds.

"An' it jumped on me with its claws out an' its

mouth open an' I put up my hands an' caught it by the neck while it was jumpin', an' squeezed it, clawin' my face with its claws, till it was dead."

"William, come in and have your medicine."

William's elation dropped from him, and he dragged himself indoors, looking not at all like a big game hunter, but like a small boy, about to be given, despite his protests, a very nauseous draught. The doctor was an old enemy of William's, and William suspected —with some justification—that he made his medicine a good deal nastier than it need be.

He returned, twisting his face into almost incredible contortions, and gave the imaginary audience a revised account of his wounds. They were due now to a struggle with a villain who had tried to poison him (William described the villain realistically) but whose dead body now lay by the precipice on which the struggle had taken place. So realistic was his description that he was surprised and slightly taken aback when, in the middle of it, the villain, whom he had just described so realistically, stopped his car at the gate and walked up to the front door, saying breezily to William:

"Well, young man, I've got a new tonic for you. I'm afraid it's rather nasty, but people who get blown up by geysers always have to have rather nasty medicine. You'll find that all the medicine books say so."

William affected a haughty silence, and revised his account of the struggle with the villain in order to give the villain a more terrible and lingering death.

But he was to go to school the next day, and he couldn't help feeling cheerful at the prospect. William was no student but he soon tired of his own company.

"GO ON! TELL US HOW IT HAPPENED," PIPED
UP A VOICE AT THE BACK.

And so the next morning he was setting forth
blithely on his way to school.

Considering the solitary bandage that now adorned
his brow to be inadequate, he had purloined all the

B

other rolls of bandage from his mother's medicine chest, and stopped in the wood to put them on. Generous in all he undertook, he rather overdid it and, when he had finished, his head, face, and neck, were completely swathed in thick white rolls, leaving only small gaps for his eyes and mouth. The effect when he reached school was, however, flattering. In a muffled voice he explained that the whole of his face except his eyes and mouth was blown away. The crowd, clustered around him in the cloakroom, hung breathless upon his words. Suggestions and queries were hurled at him from all sides.

"What're you goin' to do? I'd wear a mask. I'd get a funny one that'd make people laugh."

"Don't see how your eyes stick in if there's nothin' for 'em to stick to," said another.

"I bet you twopence they fall out when he starts to run," offered a youthful sportsman who was gazing at William with eyes that themselves seemed in danger of falling out.

"Go on! Tell us about it," piped up a voice at the back.

Nothing loth, William proceeded to tell them about it. The muffled intonation of his voice added to the impressiveness of his story. When he described his feelings as he shot through the air amid the débris of the falling house, his listeners drew gasps of delight, and it was not till one of the more literal-minded said, "Well, I don't see how your house can be blown up an' your father and mother killed, 'cause I saw the house *an'* your father an' mother only yesterday," that William realised how far he had surrendered himself to his imagination.

"Huh!" he said scornfully, "they can build up

houses jolly quick nowadays, an' all I said was they were *nearly* dead."

A dozen voices readily informed him that, on the contrary, he had definitely told them that they were not only dead, but blown to bits.

"All right," began William in the aggressive tone of one who challenges his enemies to mortal combat, then, remembering the rather precarious nature of his bandaging, changed his tone to that of a patient sufferer.

"All right! Anyone who thinks I'm a liar, say so, and as soon as my face grows again I'll lick him."

Everyone present promptly said so, less from a real objection to William's flights of fancy than from a conscientious readiness to accept any challenge that was going.

"All right!" said William. "Soon as my face grows again I'll lick the whole lot of you."

The bandages that he had put on were already beginning to yield to the force of gravity, and he was glad to escape to the schoolroom, where, under cover of his desk, he could partially readjust them. But there seemed to be more in putting on a bandage than he had realised. The one that his mother had put on was still quite firm, but the others, put on by himself, seemed to be loosening and unwinding themselves in a most curious manner. By the end of the first lesson (a French lesson) they had worked themselves down so that they completely covered his eyes and he had to part them to look at the board. The French master glared at him suspiciously, but, on the principle of letting sleeping dogs lie, forbore to question him on his strange appearance. During the next lesson—

a Latin lesson—the bandage had slipped down over his mouth, completely gagging him.   Despite his struggles he was unable to answer two very simple questions that the Latin master asked him, and was given a detention. "Just like him," he muttered ferociously into his gag, "expectin' people blown to bits to answer his silly questions."

By the next lesson—Maths.—the gag had slipped down till it enveloped his throat, and the Maths. master, who was rather short-sighted, bellowed:

"What d'you mean by coming to class wearing a muffler?   Go to the cloakroom and take it off at once!"

William, whose face was aching from the strain of trying to keep up a bandage that was determined to come down, was not sorry to retire and divest himself of it.   It had already blinded, choked and nearly throttled him, and he was feeling now a natural animosity towards it.   The original bandage, arranged by his mother, was still tight and comfortable and must suffice for the present to win him the interest and sympathy that he felt he needed.   After taking off the bandage he amused himself for the rest of the time that the Maths. lesson would occupy by bandaging a Rugby football that he found in the cloakroom, and imagining it to be the doctor's battered head.   "Yes," he addressed it sternly, "p'raps you'll *think* a bit before you start tryin' to poison me nex' time."   He returned to the class-room, just as the Maths. lesson came to an end.   The Maths. master was glad to have been freed of William's presence (William was an expert in the art of not understanding) and accepted William's explanation that it had taken a long time to get the muffler off without comment.

Immediately the master had disappeared, the class set upon William in righteous indignation and disappointment at finding his face complete with all the usual features.

"Well, it's grown again," William defended himself. "I can't help my face bein' so strong an' healthy that it grows again quicker than other people's would. I felt it'd grown again an' that's why I took the bandage off. I've got *one* on still, haven't I? My head's still blown away, isn't it? Well, I'll tell you what it felt like bein' blown up through the air——"

But the class didn't want to hear what it felt like being blown up through the air. It had, in fact, already heard it several times. What it wanted now was vengeance on William for having a complete face after having claimed to have only a partial one. It was surrounding him with hostile intent, and William, the lust of battle rising within him, had already shot out his fist at the ringleader, and received the ringleader's fist in his eye, when a boy put his head in at the class-room door and said:

"I say! Have you heard the news? Ole Markie's goin' to get married."

William and the rest of the class at once forgot the incipient struggle, and crowded round the bearer of the news.

"*Markie!*" "Who told you?" "Who's he goin' to marry?" "Go on!" "Tell your grandmother." "Goin' to get married myself."

But the news was authentic. Markie (whose real name was Mr. Marks and who was the headmaster of the school) had told the sixth form that he was going to be married. He had even told them to whom he was going to be married.

"He says it's to Miss Finch, an' he'll be married at the end of the term."

Then the master who was to take them for the next lesson arrived, scattered the crowd by a ferocious bellow, and leapt headlong into the exports of Australia.

When "break" came, the class gathered together to discuss the matter. They were doubtful as to what attitude to adopt over the question, till a lugubrious-looking boy, who had joined the school the term before, enlightened them.

"I know what it's like to have a headmaster what's married," he informed them mournfully, "we had one at the last school I went to. She sneaked to him all the time about everything. She was always hanging about the place, and she'd tell him whenever she saw us being rough in the streets even on Saturday or goin' out untidy or anything like that, an' then he'd swish us. She was always sneaking an' gettin' us swished. She'd even sneak about when she saw us fighting in our own gardens."

The faces of the Outlaws registered blank horror. They considered the headmaster to be a veritable Nero on the school premises, but there was no doubt at all that there were redeeming features about him. Away from the school premises, he ignored his flock completely. When not actually on duty he was so absent-minded that he had on one occasion come upon William in the act of trespassing in his garden, and had passed him by with a cursory glance without even realising that he was there at all. You could meet him in the streets or lanes of the village, and it did not matter how dirty or untidy you were, it did not matter what nefarious practice you were engaged in, you could be quite sure that, even if he saw you at all (which was unlikely), he would fail to recognise you as a member of his school, and that, even if (by miracle) he recognised you as a member of his school, he would have completely forgotten the incident by the next morning. Outside the school gates you had nothing to fear from old Markie. He spent his spare time writing books on such unnecessary branches of knowledge as Roman Britain and Roman Roads and Roman Law, books which were thought much of in scholastic circles but that only increased the Outlaws' already firm conviction of his insanity. And now the comparative immunity from persecution that existed outside the school gates was to cease. Even now, as they proceeded along the village street, their scuffling and pushing of each other (proceedings indispensable to their progress anywhere) was mechanical and half-hearted. Already a forbidding if shadowy female seemed to glare at them severely from the hedgerows as they passed.

"What's she like?" said Henry at last dejectedly. "This Miss Finch, I mean."

"I know where she lives," said Douglas, "let's go'n' look at her."

They followed Douglas to a small gabled house at the other end of the village, and stood gazing in fearful curiosity over the gate. There were no signs of any occupant. "Let's go'n' look through a window," whispered Ginger. Cautiously they opened the gate, entered the garden, and approached the window. Immediately it was flung up, and a middle-aged woman, tall, angular and very severe-looking—the embodiment of all their worst forebodings—appeared in the aperture.

"How *dare* you come into my garden!" she said

sternly. "Go away at once. And shut the gate. I shall report you to your headmaster." So cowed in spirit were the Outlaws that they crept away without any sign of defiance. William put his tongue out at her, certainly, but in such a way that she could not possibly see him.

In the road they stood and drew breaths of horror and dismay.

"Crumbs!" said Henry. "It's goin' to be worse than what he said."

The lady had now appeared at her gate.

"Go away at once!" she commanded again, "and don't hang about like that in the road just by my gate. And what do you *mean* by going about in such an untidy dirty state! Look at that boy's stocking hanging right over his boots. I shall speak to your headmaster most *strongly* about you."

The Outlaws trailed dejectedly down the road till out of sight of the cottage, then stood and stared at each other again in speechless horror.

"*Well!*" said Ginger at last, "we might as well be *dead* once he's married to *her*!"

Life seemed to stretch before them—an arid desert inhabited by gaunt and irascible females.

"She might die of something before they get married," said Douglas, snatching feebly at the only ray of hope that he could see.

"People like that don't die," said Henry. "Not till they're so old they can't go on living any longer. You never find a person like *that* dying when you want 'em to."

Then William spoke slowly and thoughtfully.

"He's not *axhully* married to her yet. People don't *always* get married just 'cause they're engaged."

"All the people I've known did," said Douglas.

"Well, you've not known everyone in the world, have you?' said William crushingly.

"GO AWAY AT ONCE!" SHE COMMANDED, "AND DON'T HANG ABOUT LIKE THAT JUST BY MY GATE."

Then the church clock struck five and the Outlaws separated, still slowly, still dejectedly, for tea.

William ate his tea with such an air of abstraction that his mother asked solicitously if his head was worse.

William, whose head was now completely well but who always liked to make the most of that note of solicitude in his mother's voice, said that it was much worse, and accepted with an air of patient suffering the chocolate biscuits she gave him to comfort him.

"Mother," he said as he nibbled them. "Ole Markie's going to be married."

"Mr. Marks, dear," his mother corrected him conscientiously. "Yes, so I've heard."

"To Miss Finch."

"Yes, so I heard."

"Mother, have all the people you've known engaged got married?"

"No, dear," said his mother.

"Who didn't?"

"I had a friend who didn't."

"Why didn't she?"

"She found out that he drank. She married someone else afterwards."

"I shouldn't mind her marrying someone else as long as she didn't marry *him*," said William.

"William, what *are* you talking about!"

"Nothin'," said William. "My head's gone worse again. Can I have a few more chocolate biscuits?"

"Yes," said his mother, opening the tin, "but if it's really worse I'd better ring up the doctor."

"Oh, no," said William indistinctly, as he hastily made sure of his biscuits, "it's not bad enough to bother *him*. I don't like botherin' him. He's so busy. It's gone all right again, anyway, now, quite sudden."

Munching his biscuits, he went down to meet the Outlaws at the old barn. They were sitting waiting for him—a depressed and mournful-looking little group. But, as soon as they saw him coming, they knew that he had a plan.

* * * * *

William's head had so completely healed the next morning that it needed all his cunning to make his mother bandage it.

"I'm frightened of it getting bad again," he said. "I don't want to give you any more trouble with it. That's all I'm thinkin' about. I might fall on somethin' an' then, if there was a bandage on it, it might stop it gettin' bad again."

She yielded at last and bandaged his head, inspecting with dismay the black eye that was the result of that single interchange of blows with the boy who had objected to the sudden and fully featured reappearance of his face.

Last night the black eye had been almost indistinguishable from the surrounding grime of his countenance, but this morning it had reached the perfection of its development, and gave him a sinister and battered look.

"William," said his mother, "you've *surely* not been fighting again?"

"Fighting?" said William in innocent surprise. "No, I've not been fighting. A boy happened to have his hand out, an' I happened to walk into it with my face, that's all. I cun't help his hand bein' out, could I?"

William, who usually disliked having to bear about on his countenance visible proofs of the prowess of his enemies, seemed on this occasion rather pleased by his black eye than otherwise. He inspected its rich plum colour in the looking-glass with a satisfied smile. After the experience of yesterday he forbore to decorate his

person with any more bandages, but he cautiously
pulled down his mother's bandage till it joined his black
eye and thus increased his shattered appearance. On
reaching school he first looked anxiously at his adversary of yesterday, and was relieved to find that his
eye was enclosed in a plum-coloured circle. William
needed his own black eye for his Plan, but honour
demanded that the adversary also should wear one.

The Outlaws looked at William with pleased interest.

"You look fine!" said Ginger. "Couldn't you do
something else to yourself, though? Get a tooth
knocked out or something."

"Get one knocked out yourself," said William, stung
by this suggestion. "Anyone'd think you wanted me
dead."

"No," said Ginger, "we don't want you *quite* dead,
but we'd do with you a bit more knocked about than
what you are."

"Oh you would, would you?" said William, squaring
up to him, "well, come an' knock me then." But
Ginger declined the invitation.

"No," he said simply, "I don't want to get knocked
about myself. It's *you* that's supposed to be that."

"Well, I'm knocked about enough," said William,
"an' I'm not goin' to get knocked about any more, not
for anyone. Whose plan was it, anyway? Well, if
it was my plan, I'm the one to say how much I've got
to be knocked about for it, an' I say I'm knocked about
enough. I only *thought* of it 'cause I *was* knocked about
to start with. I didn't mean that I was goin' to get
any extra knockin' about. If you want any more
knockin' about than what I've got already you can
go'n' get it yourself."

Despite this determination to acquire no more

knocking about, William accidentally fell in the playground during "break," and acquired a cut down the side of his face that made his appearance, from an artistic point of view, completely satisfying. Any further bruises or scratches would have been gilding the lily.

The Outlaws hid their delight at this fresh accident as well as they could, for William was getting to be a little touchy about his appearance.

"I don't want to go about lookin' like the sort of person what's been licked in a fight," he grumbled. "I can't tell *everyone* that the geyser did the bandage, an' the playground the cut, an' that the boy what gave me a black eye's got one himself, an' I'm jolly well sick of people askin' silly questions about it."

But the Outlaws tactfully brought the conversation round to the question of Mr. Marks's *fiancée* and William's spirits rose again. The subject was still being discussed animatedly on all sides, and William's contribution to the conversation was a meaning and mysterious snort.

"Huh!" he said. "Yes, *when* he's married. Yes, *when* he's married. Huh! Yes, *when* he's married. ... Huh!"

He was prevented from continuing this cryptic comment by someone who offered to sit on his head if he didn't shut up. William, who did not consider his head at present a fit subject for sitting on, spiritedly accepted the challenge for the next day.

"You can try it then," he said and added, "an' it won't be *mine* that'll get sat on, let *me* tell *you*."

It was a half-holiday, and immediately after lunch the Outlaws made their way to a lonely part of the lane that led to Miss Finch's house. Their proceedings there would have surprised an observer, had an observer been present, especially if the observer had been aware of their characters. For William, the haughty leader, allowed himself to be laid in the road and his face rubbed in the dust. The result was horrible. The bandaged head, the black eye, the cut on his cheek, looked, beneath the covering of dust, more sinister even than before. It was Ginger—somewhat of an artist despite his appearance—who suggested the making of "tear marks" through the dust, and carefully imprinted them with a twig dipped in water from the ditch. Then they stepped back and gazed at the result, drawing deep sighs of satisfaction. Only his expression needed a little further embellishment.

"Try'n' look more scared," said Ginger. "Crumbs! That's *fine*!" as William assumed an expression of exaggerated misery. "Come on! Let's go now quick while he looks jus' like that."

Silently they hastened down the road, William preserving his woebegone expression with something of an effort.

At the gate they stopped, and Ginger, drawing himself up with the air of one who braces himself for a deed of daring, walked to the front door, and knocked on it smartly.

Miss Finch opened the door, and her severe expression grew yet more severe.

"What do you want?" she demanded sharply.

Ginger doffed his cap with a touching air of courtesy and humility.

"Please," he said, "may our friend come in an' rest? He's not feelin' well an' he says he can't walk any further."

"Certainly——" began the lady, and it was obvious

that she was going to end the sentence with an emphatic negative, when her eye fell upon William, who was clinging to the gate post in an attitude of exhaustion and suffering that was drawing glances of admiration from Douglas and Henry. Her mouth dropped open suddenly. Even from the front door William looked a horrible spectacle.

"Good Heavens!" she gasped, "what's happened to him?"

"Oh, he's all right," said Ginger. "I mean, he'll be all right if you'll jus' let him come in an' rest a minute. He's—he's quite all right."

Douglas and Henry were already supporting William's drooping form up the path.

"Bring him in here," ordered Miss Finch, flinging open the door of her little morning-room. Her eyes gleamed with a light that betokened less sorrow for the sufferer than joy at the thought of punishing his assailant, whoever it might be.

"Let him lie down on the sofa," she said.

Ginger and Henry carefully laid the form of William on a sofa. William was rather overdoing his expression of patient suffering. He looked now less like a fainting boy than a boy who was suffering from an acute and active bilious attack. But the lady suspected nothing. She turned her searching glance upon Ginger.

"Who has done this?" she said.

"Oh—he'll be all right," said Ginger evasively. "No one did it—I mean—I couldn't tell—I mean—he'll be all right when he's had a bit of a rest."

A blind imbecile would have known that Ginger had something to hide. The lady's eyes gleamed yet more brightly. Her breath came quickly like that of a hunter hot on the scent.

"*Who*," she said, "has knocked this poor boy about in this brutal fashion?"

William opened his eyes, and spoke in a faint suffering voice.

"Don't tell her, Ginger," he said.

The lady's eyes became like spear thrusts.

"I *insist* on you telling me," she said to Ginger.

"No one did it," said Ginger. "It was just an accident."

WILLIAM SPOKE IN A FAINT, SUFFERING VOICE.
"DON'T TELL HER, GINGER," HE SAID.

"I INSIST ON YOU TELLING ME," THE LADY SAID TO
GINGER.

"Rubbish!" said the lady.

William again opened his eyes and spoke in the faint suffering voice.

"Don't tell her, Ginger. He—he didn't mean to do it."

"*Who* was it?" demanded the lady.

"It was no one," said Ginger. "I mean—it was an accident. He—he got his head hurt in an explosion, and he got the cut on his face by falling on the playground."

Ginger thought this was rather clever. They wouldn't be able to say afterwards that he hadn't told the truth.

"Don't talk such *nonsense!*" snapped the lady. "I shan't let any of you go out of this room till you've told me who has ill-treated that poor boy."

Once more William opened his eyes and murmured: "Don't tell her," adding this time, "He's all right when he's not been drinking."

"*Who* is?" demanded Miss Finch.

"Mr. Marks," said William as if the words had slipped out, then as if hastily trying to cover them up. "No, I didn't mean he did it. At least—he didn't mean to hurt me as much as this. It's—it's all right. He'd just been drinkin' an' he never knows what he's doin' when he's been drinkin'."

"He knocked me about like this last week," said Ginger sadly, "after he'd been drinkin'. He bashed my head in and knocked me down too. I just happened to get in his way when he'd been drinking. He's *quite* all right," he added as if anxious to emphasise every redeeming feature of the case, "when he's sober."

"Only he's hardly ever sober," put in Douglas sorrowfully.

Miss Finch sat down heavily in the nearest chair and gaped at the four boys, bereft of speech. When the power of speech returned to her, she gasped:

"You're not—you're not talking of Mr. Marks, the headmaster of the Grammar School."

"Yes," said Ginger simply, "we are."

"B—b—but it's *impossible*," said the lady in the tone of one who, though deeply shocked, is quite ready to believe the worst.

"I asked you not to tell her," murmured William pathetically. "He only gets really drunk about every other day. There's gen'rally a day in between when he's not drunk."

"But," gasped the lady, "it's impossible that this should have been going on in our midst and we not know!"

"*We* all knew," said Ginger, "but we've sort of kept it a secret till now."

"You mean—all the boys know?"

"Yes," said Ginger.

"And you have been *terrorised* into keeping this secret?"

"Yes," said Ginger.

"It's dreadful," said the lady, "*dreadful!* But it's quite possible. I've lived in the world long enough to know that *nothing* of that sort is impossible." She looked out of the window and suddenly said, "Wait a minute," and disappeared, to re-enter a few seconds later followed by a tall gloomy-looking man.

"I just saw Mr. Potter passing," she said, "so I thought I'd call him in. He's on the governing board of the School and I think that he ought to know about it."

The Outlaws gazed in silent dismay from Miss Finch

to the tall, gloomy-looking man. Things were not taking quite the turn that they had meant them to take. Miss Finch was talking with animated severity to the newcomer.

"And that poor boy's been terribly knocked about by him. They say that it's been going on for a long time, and that, of course, the whole school knows about it, but everyone has been too frightened to report it. Something must be done about it at once, Augustine. There's a meeting of the governing body to-morrow, isn't there? You must bring the whole thing to light. There's no doubt about it all. These boys didn't want to tell me. I had to drag it out of them. The man was intoxicated to-day and knocked this boy about in a most brutal manner for no reason at all. Just look at his injuries. They speak for themselves, don't they? You must get rid of the man at once. He must be confronted with this boy and with the evidence these boys have given me to-day. I know their names and where they live. They must be brought before the governing body to tell them what they have told me. It's a disgraceful state of things, and it must be put a stop to at once." She turned to the Outlaws who were staring at her, speechless with horror. "You may leave the matter entirely in my hands, boys. This gentleman is my *fiancé* and he will see that the matter is brought before the governing body to-morrow."

William spoke in a voice that was faint and far away.

"B-but—I thought that—that——"

"That what, my dear boy?"

"That you were goin' to marry ole M-Mr. Marks?"

"I? What *nonsense*! Of *course* not! Now, my dear boys, go away at once. This is a very serious matter and I must arrange with Mr. Potter exactly how to tackle it in order to remedy it quickly and sharply. I am beginning to think that the best thing to do is to have him arrested at once for assault on this boy——"

Nightmare bonds of horror held William.

"Please," he burst out wildly, "please he didn't do it! We made it up because——"

"*Nonsense!* Don't start that all over again. I know when you're telling the truth and when you're merely trying to excuse this man because you're afraid of him. And you are much to blame for not having reported the matter before. Augustine, I'm inclined to think that the best thing to do would be for us to go to the police about it to-night. That a habitual drunkard should remain in charge of children a *minute* longer is—— Will you stop talking, boys! I can't hear a word you say. Turn them out, Augustine. That boy seems quite well now."

The Outlaws found themselves deposited on the doorstep, and the door shut firmly behind them. They staggered down to the road as if in a trance.

"*Well!*" said Ginger at last. "*Now* you've done it."

"You're always having plans an' they're always turning out like this," said Henry.

"Well, they said he was marryin' her," said William with spirit. "I can't help it. It was a jolly good plan."

"They'll go to the police an' to ole Markie an' our fathers," said Henry, "an' we'll get swished by our fathers *an'* by ole Markie an' as like as not put in prison as well."

"I shouldn't mind bein' put in prison," said Douglas, contemplating the stormy existence that lay immediately ahead of him. "You'd get a bit of peace there, anyway."

"Well I don't care, it was a jolly good plan," said William, "an' it'd've been all right, if——"

"S'pose she comes out after us now," said Ginger. "Let's get right away."

The Outlaws set off at a run, feeling that already the terrible woman was on their track. Rounding a bend in the road, they collided with a girl—collided so heavily that William and the girl sat down suddenly in the road. . . . She was an extremely pretty girl with dark eyes, dimples, and dark curling hair. She didn't seem at all annoyed at being knocked over in the road. She only dimpled deliciously, and said that it didn't matter in the least. Then she sat on the grass on the roadside, smiled up at them and said: "Now I'm down here it's so nice and cool and comfortable, I think I'll have a rest."

Her smile was very pleasing to the Outlaws. It lulled their minds to temporary forgetfulness of the unpleasantness that lay behind and the still greater unpleasantness that lay ahead. They sat down on the grass with her, and, without knowing exactly how or why, they found themselves talking to her about Red Indians and Pirates. They even found themselves telling her of the special places where they fished and hunted, and exactly what they were going to do when they were robber chiefs and had conquered the world. She was the sort of girl to whom one tells things. So sympathetic was she that they not only forgot that she was grown up, but they also forgot the sea of troubles on which they were afloat. She knew all about Red Indians and could tell them a lot of things about them that they didn't know. She quite understood their ambition to conquer the world. She said that once she'd decided to do the same herself. She knew now, of course, that she couldn't, but she wished them better luck. She showed them a way to tie knots that they had not known before. And when the subject wandered to butterflies and caterpillars, she seemed to know everything there was to know about butterflies and caterpillars.

When finally she gathered up her parcels and said, "Well, I suppose I ought to be going," the Outlaws awoke from a pleasant dream to nightmare reality.

"What's the matter?" she said, as she saw the expressions of dejection and apprehension that had settled upon all their countenances.

They didn't mean to tell her but somehow it all came out. "An' we heard he was gettin' married——"

"An' someone knew a head that'd been married an' she was on at them all the time, tellin' tales an' gettin' 'em swished."

"An' William's mother knew a woman what'd not married a man she was engaged to 'cause he drank."

"An' we went to this Miss Finch, an' told her that he drank, an' that he'd knocked William down an' done that to his head an' face. He happ'ned to have 'em done so it all seemed to fit in."

"We thought she'd jus' tell him she wouldn't marry him."

"'Stead of that she said she'd never been goin' to marry him an' she fetched in a man she said was a governor an' they're goin' to the police——"

"An' she wouldn't *listen* to us when we tried to tell her the truth an'——"

"An' we're goin' to get into the biggest row we've ever got into in our lives——"

"'Cause he *doesn't* drink an'——"

The girl sat up and wiped her eyes.

"Oh how funny," she said, "how deliciously funny! But you needn't worry about that at *all*. It's *quite* all right. I'll go to see her now, and I'll explain everything, and I *promise* you won't get into a row."

"Yes," said William gloomily. "That's all very well. But we're sure to get into a row. You don't know ole Markie."

"I *do* know ole Markie," said the girl, "and I *promise* you won't get into a row. You see," the delicious dimples peeped out again, "I'm no relation of hers, but I'm the Miss Finch he's going to marry."

CHAPTER III

WILLIAM AND THE YOUNG MAN

WILLIAM sat on the top of the 'bus, humming discordantly to himself. Whenever his eye fell upon a hatless head in the road below, he would take an acorn from his pocket and give careful aim. He did it absentmindedly, almost mechanically. When an acorn fell on to the very top of the head (where he always aimed), he felt no joy or exultation, only the impersonal satisfaction of the artist who knows that his work is good. It was his usual way of beguiling the time on a 'bus journey. Only a completely bald head could rouse him to any real enthusiasm. His victims, rubbing their heads (an acorn can sting more than anyone who has not experienced it can realise) and glaring angrily about them, saw only a 'bus passing peacefully on its way, and, on the top, a small boy gazing wistfully into the distance.

Having reached the point of the road at which he meant to alight, William slid down the stairs using the hand rails only and not touching the steps with his feet (a point of honour this), and, before the conductor knew what he was about, had sprung from the 'bus on to the road, where he rolled over and over in the mud.

William was trying to learn to alight from a 'bus when it was going at full speed. His attempts showed more courage than science as he always leapt free of it, both feet together in the attitude of one taking a "long jump." The results were, of course, painful, but William persisted in this method, with a rather pathetic trust in the precept "Practice makes perfect."

The driver of a motor car that was following the 'bus avoided his prostrate form by swerving wildly, then slowed down to bestow on him some picturesque home truths. William picked himself up, much cheered by the episode and by the addition of a few forceful terms to his vocabulary, and went on his way to the spot where he had arranged to meet Ginger, Douglas and Henry. He found them waiting for him.

"Crumbs!" said Ginger, eyeing his mud-covered form with interest. "Wherever have you been?"

William, finding an unsuccessful descent from a 'bus too tame an adventure, invented another one in which a band of robbers had attacked him in the wood, and, after a spirited contest, had fled from him. None of them, of course, believed him, but William's adventures were always worth hearing. After listening with interest to his account (the robber chief's conversation was especially interesting, because William had enriched it with the gems dropped by the motorist) they turned to the real business of the day, which was a Hare and Hounds race. It had been arranged that William was to be Hare and the others the Hounds. William had filled his pockets with torn paper, and the others had also brought contributions which they stuffed into his stockings and down his waistcoat.

"We're jolly well not goin' to have you sayin' you'd no more paper," said Ginger.

"Mine's an ole Latin exercise book," said Douglas,

"so that oughter be easy to see 'cause it's nearly all red ink."

After partaking of refreshment in the shape of a bottle of liquorice water and a bagful of crusts of sandwiches that Henry had begged from the cook, who was making preparation for a tea party, they began the race.

William ran happily along the road, scattering his paper as he went. He was optimistic, and was convinced that the hounds had been misled by a detour he had made at the beginning of the race and were already miles away from him in the wrong direction. It came, therefore, as an unpleasant surprise, when he had been running about twenty minutes, to hear their voices quite close behind him. He stopped, panting, and looked around. A bend in the road hid them from view, and they could not have seen him yet. But the road was very long and very straight, and it was quite clear that before he reached the end of it they would have sighted him. There wasn't even a ditch, and on either side of the road was open country. Suddenly he noticed a lane on his left. It led between trees and grass, then curved quickly out of sight. William sped down it with energy suddenly renewed. It wasn't till he had sped down it for some distance and had put several bends of it between him and the main road, that he began to suspect that he was trespassing on someone's private property. It wasn't till he rounded a huge clump of rhododendron bushes and charged full tilt into an elegant party having tea on a terrace in front of a palatial mansion, that he fully realised what had happened. The lane had not been a lane. It had been the park entrance to one of the stately homes of England. It was too late to turn to flee, even if he had

had sufficient breath and presence of mind. He stood there panting and gazing at the assembled party in horror. The horror with which William gazed at the assembled party, however, was as nothing to the horror with which the assembled party gazed at William, and their horror was on the whole the better justified. For William was not such a figure as one instinctively associates with the stately homes of England. His person and clothing still bore ample traces of his flying descent from the 'bus. His career as a hare had left visible marks upon him. He had lost his cap. His hair was an impenetrable jungle. Perspiration had mingled with the dust on his face and given him a wild and travel-stained appearance. He had, moreover, scratched one side of his face extensively in getting through a hedge. The party consisted of four elderly ladies of patrician appearance and one bored-looking young man. On the tea-table, William noticed, was such a chocolate cake as one seldom meets with outside one's dreams. A tall lady with an eagle nose, who was evidently the mistress of the stately home, rose and fixed William with an outraged eye.

"How *dare* you come trespassing in my garden like this, you naughty, dirty little boy?" she said majestically. "Do you know that I've a good mind to send for the police? Who's your father?"

Before William had time to answer (he was going to say that he was an orphan) the young man had leapt from his chair with a welcoming smile.

"By Jove, old chap," he said, "here you are at last! I've been expecting you all afternoon. This is a friend of mine, aunt, whom I asked to tea. You know that you very kindly said that any friend of mine would be welcome."

The patrician-looking lady with the eagle nose blinked and swallowed. The young man was shaking William warmly by the hand, and drawing him down into an empty basket-chair near the table, where he continued to talk to him affectionately.

"A long walk from the station isn't it, old chap? I'm sure you're hungry. Have some tea."

Despite his odd behaviour the young man appeared to be a young man of sound enough sense. By "tea" he meant chocolate cake. He did not offer William the insult of passing him the bread and butter. He passed him the chocolate cake and continued to pass it at very frequent intervals till no more was left. The ladies resumed their interrupted conversation, throwing occasional glances of dislike and dismay at William. So surprised had William been by his mysterious welcome, so utterly taken up by the heavenly flavour of the chocolate cake, that he completely forgot his function of hare till the last crumb of the chocolate cake had vanished. Then, just as he remembered it, the young man said. "Like to have a look round the kitchen garden?" and William promptly forgot it again. The ladies' conversation died away into dumb horror, as they watched the form of William setting off to the kitchen garden with his new friend. William's stockings were working down, and small pieces of torn-up papers were dropping from them, marking his trail, as though they continued to remember that he was a hare despite his own forgetfulness. His waistcoat, also, as if fortified by the chocolate cake, was remembering his duties for him, and dropping torn-up paper conscientiously across the velvet lawn.

"What—what an *extraordinary* child!" said one lady faintly.

"So—so *odd* that he should be Anthony's friend," said another.

"Sometimes," said Anthony's aunt impressively, "sometimes I have serious doubts of Anthony's sanity."

Meantime the young man had piloted William to the kitchen garden, and let him loose among the gooseberry bushes. The gooseberries were of the large, green, succulent kind, favoured by the stately homes of England, and the chocolate cake was already only a faint and distant memory. The young man was leaning negligently against the wall watching him.

"I fear," he was saying, "that I owe you an explanation and an apology. What is your name, by the way?"

"William," said William shortly and indistinctly from the middle of a gooseberry bush.

"Well, William, I'll explain the situation as well as I can. You see I'm staying with my aunt. I stay with my aunt every summer. And I find her very trying. She preaches, William. She preaches all day and every day. She hardly stops even to take nourishment. She preaches on industry, and thrift and godliness and other similar subjects. The only reason why I haven't murdered her is because I'm not sure whether she's made her will yet. And I hatched a little plot with a friend of mine. She's always describing to me the type of man I should choose for my friend—a sort of blend of Little Lord Fauntleroy and Sir Charles Grandison—and she's often said that any friend of mine would be welcome here, so we hatched this little plot. He's quite inoffensive-looking naturally, but he can make himself up as the biggest bounder that ever came out of Creation. He's got a special suit for it fashioned in a check that you can hear ten miles away, and he's got a special bowler hat for it and rings and tiepin, and, with his nose reddened, he's the real, real thing. I told my aunt that a friend of mine might possibly be arriving for tea, and we'd arranged that he should don his bounder's outfit—red nose and all—and arrive. I was looking forward to it more than I've ever looked forward to anything in my life, when I got a letter from him this morning saying that he's down with flu and can't come. I was sitting at tea feeling as blue as the ocean waves, when suddenly I saw them all looking at someone with the very expressions with which I had dreamed of their looking at my friend. And so on the spur of the moment I claimed you as my friend. That is the whole story. You aren't offended, I hope?"

"Oh, no," said William, but he spoke distantly. He could not help feeling that the rôle he played in the situation was not a heroic one.

"It has been an unqualified success," went on the young man in a propitiating manner as if anxious to dispel the coldness from William's manner. "I have enjoyed the afternoon every bit as much as if my real friend had come, and I feel much indebted to you. Come over to this wall. There are some jolly fine nectarines on it."

"Thanks awfully," said William, his haughtiness melting.

The young man took him round the garden, pointing out the finest specialities, and, by the time they emerged from the last hothouse, William was conscious of a distant sensation of internal congestion (a rare sensation for William) and of a feeling of unqualified cordiality towards the young man.

Wandering happily among the raspberry bushes, William saw that the young man was watching the ground with interest and became aware for the first time of the trail of paper that marked his track all round the kitchen garden, in and out of the hothouses, and finally accompanied him to the raspberries. A largish piece of paper containing the words *Pax tenavit* (Douglas's rendering into Latin of "He held his peace") heavily underlined in red ink, was in the act of floating gracefully to the ground from beneath his waistcoat.

"What on *earth*——" began the young man.

William looked about him in dismay. He felt grateful to the young man, and he had an uncomfortable suspicion that so far he had not presented himself to the young man in such a guise that the young man would remember him with that admiration and respect with which William liked to be remembered.

And now to appear as a hare who had not only broken the rules by invading private property, but had then proceeded to forget that it was a hare, would finally complete his humiliation.

Playing for time, he adopted his most mysterious expression.

"Huh!" he said. "Yes, I've gotter take clues about with me so's people can find me if I'm missing. I go into some jolly dangerous places, I do."

"Really?" said the young man with interest. "Now let me guess what you are. . . ." He frowned as if considering deeply, then his brow lightened. "I *know*!" he said. "You're a Scotland Yard man."

William hadn't been quite sure what he was when he uttered his cryptic remark, but, as soon as the young man said that he was a Scotland Yard man, he knew that he was one.

" Yes," he said, modestly, "but don't tell anyone."

"No, I won't," said the young man, "and it's a very strange thing, our meeting like this, because I'm a famous international crook. I'll tell you some of my experiences and then you tell me some of yours."

William had by this time reached the end of his redoubtable capacity for fruit eating, and they had made their way to two empty wheelbarrows that stood side by side in a corner of the kitchen garden. The young man, unlike most grown-ups, knew how to make himself comfortable in a wheelbarrow. Reclining at ease in it and smoking a pipe, he told William a few of his adventures as a famous international crook. They included leaping from an aeroplane on to an express train, and swimming the Channel under water while police hunted for him in submarines on the surface. William listened enthralled, quite forgetting his rôle as a criminal investigator. So quickly did the time pass that he could hardly believe his ears when the young man said that it was time he went to dress for dinner.

"I've enjoyed your visit tremendously," he said, "and we must meet again soon, so that you can tell me a few of your adventures. I'm afraid I've monopolised the conversation."

The young man escorted him to the gates. William was relieved to find the terrace empty. Evidently the guests had departed, and the eagle-nosed aunt had gone indoors. At the gate the young man shook hands with him cordially.

"Good-bye, old chap. Even if we have to meet in the course of our respective duties, I'm sure that we shall bear each other no ill-will."

William walked to the old barn in a dream. His thwarted hounds were awaiting him, and set upon him

o

furiously, but he soon calmed them, and in five minutes they were sitting round him listening intently, while he related to them the adventures of the famous international crook.

The next afternoon Mrs. Brown sent William to the Vicarage with a note. William's mind was still full of the young man, and he was wondering whether it would be possible to meet him again to-day and hear a few more of his adventures. His surprise was great therefore, when, on approaching the Vicarage, he saw the young man lightly shinning down a drain-pipe from one of the upper windows and disappearing through the hedge of the back garden. William stood spellbound, watching his retreating figure. Then he approached the Vicarage front door with his note. There was no reply to his knock. He went round to the back door. Again there was no reply. He knocked till he made the very saucepans in the Vicarage kitchen ring, and still there was no reply. It was quite obvious that the Vicarage was unoccupied. William walked home slowly and thoughtfully.

And the next day the Vicar, meeting William and his mother in the village, said:

"I'm feeling very much worried to-day, Mrs. Brown. I've lost a really valuable miniature—an heirloom, in fact. I can't think what's happened to it. It was in its usual place in my study yesterday morning. I'm afraid—very much afraid—that it has been stolen."

William walked on, his eyes nearly starting out of his head. In imagination he saw the young man (heavily masked) displaying the Vicar's miniature to his gang (also heavily masked) in an underground cellar. The young man had described the place so vividly to William that William felt he had actually seen it. It had secret underground passages leading into every station in London, so that the gang could escape at a moment's notice, and another leading into the middle of the Channel, so that they could when necessary swim across to France. It possessed also a maze, into which they lured those who discovered their hiding-place and from which it was impossible ever to escape. The room where the gang met had black hangings round the walls and a skull on the table at which they sat. Moreover the young man (he alone knew the secret) could switch on an electric current so that anyone entering the room while it was turned on fell dead on the threshold. So vivid in fact had been the young man's account that William was entirely out of conceit with his own Scotland Yard career (which seemed now intolerably dull) and the greatest aim of his life was to be allowed to join the young man's "gang". He supposed that he must wait until he had left school, but he would get the address of the gang's headquarters from the young man before he went away, so that he could join him immediately on leaving school.

Meeting the young man in the village street, he broached the subject. The young man was quite encouraging. He said, though, that he didn't take anyone under seventeen, and that even then William would have to work his way up from the bottom, beginning with small things like spoons and rings and gradually working up to the larger things. The young man said that he always did the big jobs—such as grandfather clocks and hall wardrobes—himself.

"But you *sometimes* do smaller things, don't you?" said William. He wanted the young man to know that he knew about the Vicar's miniature.

The young man assumed a mysterious expression and

said, "Ah-h-h!" and William was just going to tell him that he knew about the miniature, when the young man's aunt appeared suddenly at the bend of the road, and William, who knew that discretion was the better part of valour where aunts were concerned, muttered a hasty farewell and vanished.

He set off the next morning to find the young man and continue the conversation. He could not help making a détour by way of the Vicarage, however, because that pipe, down which he had seen the young man swarming so lightly, held now an irresistible glamour for him. He stood for a moment at the gate, and gazed at it with gaping eyes and mouth. While he was gazing, the front door opened, and out came the Vicar with a man whom William had never seen before. He was a tall man with a beard and piercing black eyes, and William knew at once that he was a Scotland Yard official whom the Vicar had summoned to clear up the mystery of the stolen miniature. The beard alone would have told him that even without the piercing eyes. Already William could see in imagination the scene in which this tall man stood confronting his friend and chief, tore off the beard with one hand, whipped a pistol out of his pocket with the other, and said: "And now, Alias, I think our little account is settled."

The young man had told William that, in common with many other famous criminals, he was called Alias.

The meeting made William vaguely uneasy. This man didn't look the kind of detective who is bamboozled by the criminal. Somehow he gave you the impression of being a better detective than the young man was a criminal, in spite of the skull and the black hangings. After all, it might be quite simple to cut off the electric current at the door, and, once this detective had got his men all round the place, guarding even the secret passage to the Channel, the gang wouldn't have much chance.   Probably he'd got a plan of the maze in his pocket at the moment.   William went home to lunch feeling very anxious.   And at lunch Ethel said to his mother:

"Do you know who the man is who's staying at the Vicarage?"

And his mother said:

"Yes, dear.   It's an old college friend of the Vicar's. He's a very distinguished literary man."

And William's worst fears were confirmed.   It was, of course, just what a detective who had come to stay at the Vicarage to clear up the mystery of the stolen miniature would naturally pretend to be.   That and the beard gave him away as completely as if he openly wore his Scotland Yard badge.

William felt that not a moment was to be lost.   The young man must be warned at once.   He set off at a run to Maple Court where the young man's aunt lived (the young man had told William that she knew nothing of his secret career).   At the gate he stopped, not quite sure how to proceed.   He was not, of course, on the young man's aunt's visiting list.   He was, in fact, if one may use the expression, on the reverse of her visiting list.   He certainly could not walk up to her front door and demand to see her nephew.   He decided to hang about the entrance gate unobtrusively in the hope of seeing him going in or out.   It was impossible, however, for William to do anything unobtrusively, and an indignant gardener soon came down to stop him swinging on the gate.   William stopped swinging and asked the gardener if the lady's nephew would be coming out that afternoon. The gardener recognised William with disgust as the "young rapscallion" who had been hanging about with Master Anthony in the kitchen garden last week, eating his best nectarines, and leaving a trail of dirty paper along his tidy path.

"No," he said shortly, "he's gone back to Town an' good riddance."

William heaved a sigh of relief, said, "Good riddance yourself," gate-vaulted twice over the gate, then, avoiding a well-aimed box on the ears from the gardener, set off jauntily down the road. It was all right. He might have known it would be all right. Of course the young man had recognised the Scotland Yard official at a glance, just as William had done, and had lost no time in clearing off.

The next morning he met the Vicar and his friend in the road, and was seized with such a paroxysm of mirth at the thought of the futility of their search that it was impossible to conceal it. They stood and watched him with amazement as he went on down the road, his shoulders shaking helplessly.

"What an extraordinary boy," said the Vicar's friend. "Is he always like that?"

"He is a most peculiar child," said the Vicar grimly.

"What was he laughing at?"

"I've no idea," said the Vicar and added, "I'm afraid he's inclined to be impertinent. I've noticed it on several occasions."

For the next few days William gloated triumphantly over the situation—the sleuth tracking a victim who had long ago made good his escape. And then his exultation suddenly vanished. For the victim returned. He flew through the village driving a battered

wo-seater with a large suit-case beside him, and shot
ıp the drive of Maple Court. William happened
o be in the lane just outside. His eyes grew large
vith consternation. His mouth dropped open. He
must have thought, of course, that the coast was clear
ınd that the Scotland Yard man had gone. William
must let him know at once. He mustn't stay one
moment longer. Even now it might be too late. Even
ıow—and just as William had got to that point in his
houghts, the bearded man with piercing eyes came
ound the bend in the lane, and accosted him curtly:

"Excuse me, my boy, can you tell me the way to
Maple Court?"

He, too, must have seen the young man coming from
the station and he was on his way to arrest him. Only,
ɔy a miraculous chance, he wasn't sure of the way to
the house, and, by a still more miraculous chance, it
was William he asked. William felt that he held his
friend's life in his hand, and must act promptly.

He assumed an ingratiating expression and said:

"Yes. You've come a bit out of the way. I'm
going there myself, so I'll take you."

"Thank you very much," said the Scotland Yard
man.

William concealed an exultant grin at the success
of his ruse, and the two of them set off down the lane.

"'Scuse me," said William (he remembered that
they were always very polite to each other in books till
the final moment when they faced each other with
revolvers); "'Scuse me, but what do you want to go to
Maple Court for?"

"I'm giving a lecture there," said the Scotland
Yard man.

William had to bend down to pretend to pull his

stockings up, to conceal his amusement at this. Jolly clever thing to say, of course, but they probably had special lessons at Scotland Yard in thinking of things to say like that. William had paused at a stile that led through a field up a hill.

"This is a short cut to it," he said.

The bearded man followed him guilelessly.

When they had breasted the hill, and joined another main road, and walked for some distance along it, however, he said anxiously:

"I hope we aren't making any mistake. I was told that the place was quite near the Vicarage."

"Well, they probably meant near compared with somewhere a long way off," said William. "We'll soon be there now."

They walked on in silence for another half-mile. William was wondering what to do next. It had seemed a clever trick to divert the sleuth's course, but they could not continue to walk like this all night even though they were going away from Maple Court. At some point the sleuth would realise that he was walking in the wrong direction, and, even if he didn't, England was an island and sooner or later they must reach the sea, which would, of course, give the whole show away completely. They had reached now the outskirts of Marleigh, the next village to the one where William lived, and they were walking by a low wall that bordered the roadside.

"I think that Maple Court is jus' round this corner," said William. "Would you like to sit down on the wall a minute while I go an' see?"

The sleuth sat down willingly, mopping his brow.

"I simply can't understand it," he said, "they said most distinctly only a few yards."

"HAVE YOU SEEN ANYONE COMING UP FROM THE
STATION, LITTLE BOY?" THE MAN ASKED.

"Well, you see," said William soothingly, "people
round here walk such a lot that it seems only a few
yards to them."

With that he left the sleuth and turned the corner

into the village street of Marleigh. His intention was to slip down the hill again to Maple Court and warn the young man. He thought that it would take the sleuth some time to realise that he had been tricked, and then some more time to get down to Maple Court (the sleuth was not a good walker), and that altogether there should be ample time for the young man to make his escape.

William began to hurry through the village on his way to the other field path that led down the hill. But at the first house in the village street he stopped. A large room on the ground floor was lit up. In it he could see rows and rows of people sitting facing a small platform on which was a table and an empty chair. At the door stood a tall thin man, holding a watch in his hand and looking anxiously up and down the road. Seeing William at the gate he came down to him.

"Er—have you seen anyone coming up from the station, little boy?" he said. "Our lecturer is half an hour late, and we're wondering what has happened to him."

William gasped with delight. If he could get the sleuth in here as the lecturer, the inevitable complications and explanations would delay him still further.

"Yes," he said, "I did see a man comin' along the road. I'll go'n' fetch him, shall I?"

"Thank you, my boy. If he should be the lecturer, remind him that he'd arranged to address the Marleigh Temperance Society at seven o'clock prompt. I'll go back to the audience. It's growing just a lee-tle restive."

The tall thin man disappeared. William with great cunning and presence of mind arranged a hanging branch of a beech tree to hide the legend, The Chestnuts, on the open gate, then returned to the sleuth, who was still sitting on the wall and mopping his brow.

"It's just along here," said William. The sleuth heaved a sigh of relief, and accompanied him through the gateway and up to the front door, where the tall thin man was standing to receive him.

"Delighted to see you, delighted to see you," fluted the tall thin man nervously. "Everyone is ready. Perhaps you'll step straight in here."

The sleuth followed the tall thin man into the room. William could not resist lingering by the open window to see what turn events would take. The tall thin man led the sleuth up on to the platform and said:

"And now I won't take up any more valuable time, but will ask our friend to deliver his lecture to us at once."

The sleuth stood up, took a sheaf of papers out of his pocket, and began with a moment's hesitation, "Ladies and Gentlemen . . ."

William slipped away, chuckling to himself as he imagined the sensation of rage and baffled fury that the sleuth must be feeling. To be tricked into having to address a real audience as if he were a real lecturer. . . . But the episode gave William a wholesome respect for the methods of Scotland Yard. If you came out after your prey disguised as a lecturer, you even carried a lecture in your pocket so that in an emergency you could sustain the character. They were certainly foes worth fighting. They were, of course, his, William's, foes now. They would never forgive him for having saved their victim. They would know now that he was practically a member of the young man's gang. They would always keep an eye on him. William had pleasant visions of Scotland Yard men in various disguises following him to and from school, slipping along behind him under cover of the ditch or hedge. Perhaps when the young man knew what he had done he would let him join his gang at once without waiting till he left school. . . .

He had reached the bottom of the hill now, and was running as fast as he could in the direction of Maple Court. There still wasn't a moment to be lost. The sleuth would probably make some excuse to stop lecturing when he'd done it for a few minutes, and then of course he would soon find his way back to Maple Court. The world was simply full of people ready to tell other people the way to places. . . .

At the gate of Maple Court stood the young man and the Vicar. The Vicar's being there made it rather awkward. Probably the Vicar knew by now that the young man had stolen his miniature, and was keeping an eye on him till the sleuth arrived. William must act very carefully.

"I simply can't think what's happened," the Vicar was saying. "He set off before me and I told him that it was only a few yards down the road. I can't think how he can possibly have missed it."

Suddenly the young man caught sight of William.

"Hello!" he said. "Here's my friend William. William, have you seen Mr. Chance anywhere?"

"Mr. Chance?" said William to gain time.

"Yes," said the young man, "John Chance. Surely even you have heard of John Chance?"

"No," said William to gain more time.

"I should have thought that even you——" said the young man. "Well, anyway, he's one of the most famous literary critics in England, and he's a college friend of the Vicar's, and a professor at the college that I honour with my presence, though he probably doesn't know me from Adam. Anyway the Vicar kindly arranged for him to address the Literary Society, of which my aunt is the President, on "The Drinking Songs of Britain," and he should have been here half an hour ago, and the Literary Society is getting tired of waiting."

William looked from the Vicar to the young man and a horrible certainty together with a horrible doubt entered his head. The horrible certainty was a certainty that the sleuth was not a sleuth, and the horrible doubt was a doubt whether the young man was really a criminal.

"The question is, William," said the Vicar irritably, "have you seen Mr. Chance?"

"Yes," said William, "I've just seen him in Marleigh."

"*Marleigh?*" said the Vicar. "How on earth did he get there?"

"I suppose he walked," said William after a slight hesitation.

"Well, please take us to where you saw him," said the Vicar.

William took them. The Vicar and the young man conversed amicably on the way. The Vicar was asking the young man about his studies and his college. It appeared that the young man lived a very full life at his college. He played rugger for his college and hockey for his University and rowed in his University boat. His account of his studies was vaguer and less enthusiastic. But there was something very convincing about it all, and the doubt in William's mind turned into a certainty. The young man was not a criminal. Such a life as he described would leave no time at all for criminal pursuits. He hadn't got a gang. He hadn't got an underground meeting-place, hung with black, with a skull on the table and with a secret passage to the Channel. Probably he wasn't even called Alias . . .

They had reached Marleigh now, and the Vicar had turned to William to say:

"Well, whereabouts was it you saw him?"

William pointed to The Chestnuts.

"I saw him going into that house."

"How *extraordinary*!" said the Vicar. "I do hope he hasn't lost his memory."

The Vicar and the young man went up to the front door. It was open. They entered. William realised, of course, that this was the moment for flight, but William never could resist staying to see the end of an adventure. The young man and the Vicar had stopped at the door of the room where Mr. Chance was lecturing. He was at that moment quoting the following lines:

"The peer I don't envy—I give him his bow,
    I scorn not the peasant, though never so low,
    But a club of good fellows like those that are here,
    And a bottle like this, are my glory and care."

His audience had at first been speechless with amazement, then restively indignant. This was the last straw. The tall thin man rose from the back of the room and said: "This is an outrage, sir."

Mr. Chance raised his head from his papers in surprise.

"What is an outrage?" he demanded indignantly.

"Those words you have just quoted, and the whole of your lecture," sputtered the tall thin man.

Mr. Chance was evidently annoyed by this.

"Sir, you forget yourself," he thundered.

"I do not forget myself," squeaked the tall thin man; "you are engaged to address the Temperance Society on the effects of Alcohol on the Liver and——"

"What do you mean, sir?" said Mr. Chance. "I am not addressing any Temperance Society. I never have and I never will. I detest them. I am addressing the Helicon Literary Society on the Drinking Songs of Britain and——"

It was at this point that the Vicar interrupted. While he was in the middle of his explanation, a small rabbity man arrived in a state of great nervous agitation, explaining that he had got into the wrong train at Paddington, and hadn't been able to let them know, but had come as quickly as possible. Someone kindly brought him a glass of soda-water to steady his nerves, and, taking the place just vacated by Mr. Chance, he leapt headlong into the effects of Alcohol upon the Liver.

The Vicar and the young man had drawn the deposed and bewildered lecturer down to the gate, and there hasty explanations took place. At the end of the explanations they all looked round for William. But William was nowhere to be seen. William had decided that the moment had come for him to be in bed and asleep. In fact when the Vicar called at his home a few minutes later, after leaving Mr. Chance and the young man at the gate of Maple Court, William was so soundly asleep that he resisted all his mother's attempts to awaken him.

But there had to be explanations, of course. They

took place the next morning between William, William's father, the Vicar, and the young man. William defended himself with spirit.

"How could I *know*?" he demanded passionately. "I'd seen him climbing down a drainpipe——"

"Yes, I did," agreed the young man. "I was

"YOU ARE ENGAGED TO ADDRESS THE TEMPERANCE SOCIETY ON THE EFFECTS OF ALCOHOL ON THE HUMAN RACE," SQUEAKED THE TALL, THIN MAN.

passing the Village Hall, and the Vicar came out, and said that he'd left the list of Sunday School prize winners on his study table, and the place was locked up because his wife was in town and the maids out, and

he'd forgotten to bring his keys. He'd got an unholy
rabble of Sunday School prize-winners in the Village
Hall, and daren't leave them for a second, so I said I'd

"WHAT DO YOU MEAN, SIR?" SAID MR. CHANCE. "I AM
NOT ADDRESSING ANY TEMPERANCE SOCIETY."

do my best. He told me his study window was open,
so I took the short cut across the fields and made for
that. That's true, isn't it?" he ended, turning to the
Vicar.

"In essentials," said the Vicar coldly. The Vicar

hadn't liked having his Sunday School prize winners described as an "unholy rabble."

"And then you said a miniature had been stolen," said William to the Vicar.

"I found I was mistaken," said the Vicar testily. "When I got home I found that the nail had come out of the wall and that the thing had fallen down behind the book shelves. I'd completely forgotten till you mentioned it that I'd ever thought it had been stolen."

"And you said——" went on William, turning accusingly to the young man.

"I know—I know," said the young man. "I'm afraid I let my imagination run away with me. I take the responsibility for the whole affair."

William's father, however, refused to treat the young man as responsible for the whole affair ("'Fraid of anyone his own size," muttered William bitterly) and insisted on treating William as responsible for the whole affair. But the young man gave William a ten shilling note, and said that though he wasn't a criminal he'd always thought that it would be a very exciting career, and, if William still felt the same about it when he left school, they'd seriously consider the matter.

So that William did not really regret the incident.

Nor did Mr. Chance.

On his return home he found an interviewer waiting to interview him. Mr. Chance disliked being interviewed but he looked upon it as part of the day's work. In a bored and mournful fashion he gave his views upon the modern novel, the modern play, and modern poetry. In a bored and mournful fashion he gave the interviewer his candid opinion of his own work (it wasn't flattering so the interviewer toned it down). In a bored and mournful fashion he told the interviewer that he hadn't any hobbies and that he hated gardening. Then the interviewer brought out his final question.

"And what, Mr. Chance," he said, "do you consider the greatest achievement of your life?"

The critic's bored and mournful manner vanished. He sat up, his eye gleamed, his lips curved into a proud smile.

"I consider that the greatest achievement of my life," he said, "is having delivered a lecture to the Marleigh Temperance Society on the Drinking Songs of Britain."

CHAPTER IV

THE OUTLAWS AND COUSIN PERCY

THE Outlaws always took a keen interest in the relations who came to their respective families for Christmas. Most of them, of course, came year after year, and were accepted as the inevitable accompaniments of the season, together with holly and mistletoe and having to go to church. Some, of course, were not popular, but the unpopular ones were so equally divided that each of the Outlaws was in a glass house and unable to throw stones. It was no use William's jeering at Ginger's aunt who called them "chica-biddies" and gave them toy engines for presents, because William himself had an aunt who talked to them about fairies and tried to read "Ministering Children" aloud to them. It was no use Henry's jeering at Douglas because of his aunt who wore a whole flower garden in her hat, for Douglas himself had an aunt whose two and a half yards of feather boa were still considered by her to be fashionable wear.

Uncles were much the same. William had one who laughed uproariously and senselessly at every remark any of them made, Ginger had one who continually repeated pointless jokes of his own, Henry had one who was always asking them history and geography questions, and Douglas had one who was so bad-tempered that an apple-pie bed turned him into a raving lunatic.

So familiar however were these family connections that their Christmas comings and goings aroused little interest or curiosity among the Outlaws. They were merely people to whom enough attention must be shown to ensure a tip at their departure, but who beyond that must be strenuously avoided.

The Outlaws, after much practice, had acquired great skill in gauging the exact amount of attention required for a tip in each case. They considered it inconsistent with their dignity and self respect to tender more.

This year, however, a new element entered into the situation. A cousin of Ginger's mother, whom none of them had ever seen before, by name Percy Penhurst, had written to invite himself to Ginger's for Christmas. Ginger's mother was favourably impressed by his letters.

"He's very much looking forward to seeing Ginger and his friends," she said. "He's very fond of boys."

It was William who, when told of this, succinctly remarked:

"Well, p'raps he is, but that's not the point. The point is, are boys fond of him?"

Interest rose high as the date of his arrival drew near. It was a long time since a completely new relation had come to any of their houses for Christmas. Ginger naturally was rather uneasy. He felt more responsible than he would have felt for a mere Christmas visitor, because he was having a party on Christmas Eve, and Cousin Percy's presence would make or mar it. For a "party" does not consist of one's personal friends, who accept one's queer relations with amused sympathy. It consists of acquaintances and potential enemies on the look-out for any weak spot in one's home armour. A queer relation who can be publicly mimicked is an excellent weapon of offence for months to come.

Hence the anxiety with which Ginger awaited the coming of Cousin Percy.

The reports that reached them were reassuring.

"He's wonderful with boys," said Ginger's mother, after reading the letter in which he told her what train he was coming by. "And he always gets on well with them."

It was again William who pointed out that the source of this information was obviously Cousin Percy himself. Ginger was inclined to be optimistic.

"He's been abroad anyway," he said. "So he's prob'ly shot wild animals."

Ginger's mental picture of "abroad" was a vast jungle in which intrepid hunters and fierce beasts of prey stalked each other through trackless undergrowth.

"Well, if he's shot wild animals," went on Ginger with the triumphant air of one who has proved his point, "he's sure to be a decent sort."

To this, at any rate, the Outlaws agreed.

Ginger's mother had told Ginger that he might bring William and Henry and Douglas to tea on the day of Cousin Percy's arrival, because he was so fond of boys. They had not come home, however, when he arrived. They were in the wood following tracks that they were convinced were the tracks of an elephant, but that turned out disappointingly to be marks made by one of the keepers' wives who had been taking his dinner to him. She was a large-footed woman and she wore goloshes.

Ginger's mother met them at the door on their return. She wore a smile of pleasure and relief.

"He's come, and you're *sure* to like him," she whispered, "he's *awfully* nice."

The Outlaws entered the drawing-room where Cousin Percy was awaiting them. On Ginger's face was a ray of hope that died away as his anxious eyes fell upon this Christmas guest. For a large hearty-looking man rose from a chair by the window, smiling expansively. His smile in fact was little short of devastating. It revealed every one of his teeth and he seemed to have twice as many as other people. He advanced upon the Outlaws, holding out his hands with a large, welcoming gesture.

"Well, my boys," he said, giving each one a boisterous and friendly shake, "how are you? How are you? I can't tell you how I've been looking forward to this minute. We're going to be great friends when we get to know each other, and we can't begin to do that too soon."

He then began the process known as "getting to know each other." He was revoltingly familiar, and odiously breezy. His familiarity and breeziness froze the very blood in the Outlaws' veins. And Ginger's mother, with the deplorable obtuseness of women, watched them proudly, thinking how charming Cousin Percy was, and how splendidly they were all getting on together.

After tea Cousin Percy suggested a walk, and, still talking breezily, laughing boisterously, chaffing them with unbearable familiarity, he set off, accompanied by four dejected boys.

He took them through the wood, and, with the offensive jocularity of one who thinks he is imparting instruction so subtly that the recipient has no idea that he is being instructed—a manner that the Outlaws detested beyond all others—he taught them how to tell the various trees from their shapes and twigs though there were no leaves on them. The Outlaws had not the slightest desire to be able to tell the various trees from their shapes and twigs though there were no leaves on them. Trees were not divided into oaks and beeches and elms in the Outlaws' eyes. They were divided into trees that could be climbed and trees that could not be climbed; into trees that would do for tents, or trees that would do for ships, or trees that were simply trees and nothing else. They had no wish to extend their botanical knowledge beyond that point. But Cousin Percy was breezily, slangily, affectionately instructive all through the woods. He was not disconcerted by their unresponsiveness. He didn't see it as unresponsiveness. He saw it as shy admiration. ("I'm used to being hero worshipped by boys," he had told Ginger's mother. "I don't discourage it, because it doesn't do them any harm. Does them good in fact. Gives them a sort of standard to aim at, if you know what I mean.")

Then, once out of the wood, Cousin Percy threw instruction to the winds and began to tell them stories of his boyhood. Never had boy been so brave, so innocently mischievous, so popular, and so manly, as Cousin Percy. His life had consisted in daring exploits, undertaken invariably on someone else's behalf (saving boys from drowning had been part of a normal day's work to Cousin Percy) and in sensational victories on what Cousin Percy called the "playing fields." Occasionally, it seemed, Cousin Percy had got into trouble in the fashion of ordinary boys, but on every occasion only because he was shielding the real culprit. ("I always took the punishment rather than played the sneak, my boys"), and he had frequently interfered with a big boy who was bullying a little one, however painful the consequences. ("Always protect those who are weaker than yourself, my boys.")

It was a dejected and dispirited little group that accompanied Cousin Percy homeward.

"Delightful boys," said Cousin Percy to Ginger's mother, "but at present rather shy."

Ginger's mother was surprised to hear that.

"They aren't generally shy," she said.

Cousin Percy laughed.

"I daresay it was a bit of a shock to find a grown-up so very unlike the ordinary grown up as I am. I understand boys thoroughly, you see. Oh, they won't be shy with me long."

Ginger's mother could hardly believe her ears when she heard that Ginger did not like Cousin Percy. As she said to her husband:

"It worries me, dear, because he's so wonderful with boys. One feels that a boy of the right sort would adore him. In fact he told me that they do. I'm so sorry that Ginger doesn't like him. . . . I do so hope that he'll come to like him as he gets to know him better."

But Ginger didn't come to like him as he got to know him better. In fact the better he got to know him the stronger his antipathy became. For Cousin Percy insisted on having "romps" with him, hurling pillows at him boisterously in the early morning, putting a wet sponge over his door to fall down upon him when he opened it, sewing up his pyjamas. . . .

"I've never really outgrown my own boyhood," he explained to Ginger's mother, "that's why I understand boys so well."

The other Outlaws, of course, could easily have avoided him, but they would not forsake Ginger in his hour of need, and they joined the long walks with Cousin Percy, and listened to Cousin Percy being boisterous and breezy and slyly improving. "It's the lessons they learn without knowing they're learning them that stick," he said to Ginger's mother. "A boy will learn a lesson in manliness from an entertaining story better than from any amount of sermons." So the Outlaws listened to "entertaining stories" of Cousin Percy's manly boyhood, till, as William said, "I feel the only thing I want to do is go an' sneak on someone or bully someone."

Ginger tried to stem the flow of breeziness by asking questions about Cousin Percy's travels abroad, but it seemed that Cousin Percy knew nothing of the "abroad" of Ginger's imagination. Cousin Percy's "abroad" consisted of museums and picture galleries, and, taking Ginger's question as a sign that he wished for instruction on these subjects, he proceeded to impart it. ("All boys have a natural thirst for culture," he had said to Ginger's mother, "it only wants the right person to awake it.")

He played little tricks on all of them and chided them gently for their lack of enthusiasm.

"A manly boy," he said, "is the first to appreciate a joke against himself and the first to tell it to others."

*   *   *   *   *

The Outlaws thought that they had plumbed the depth of Cousin Percy's objectionableness, but they found that they hadn't, for Cousin Percy, it transpired, had brought a little conjuring outfit with him. He showed it to them one day after tea.   The Outlaws

always stayed to tea with Ginger now. Cousin Percy
had said to Ginger's mother:

"Let them stay. It's so disappointing for the poor
chaps to have to go home and leave Ginger to have
all the fun alone."

And on the third day of his visit Cousin Percy
brought out his little conjuring outfit. The tricks
were puerile in the extreme, and accompanied by a
facetious "patter" that made the Outlaws blush for
very shame. They sat in a dejected row and counted
the moments till the exhibition should be over. They
looked upon it as a private form of torture devised
for their benefit by the loathsome Cousin Percy. It
was not till he had finished, and was packing up his
little case, that they realised what further depths of
humiliation were prepared for them. For Cousin
Percy, putting away the last string of coloured paper
(he'd produced it from an empty box, but as it had been
hanging out of his sleeve all the time the trick wasn't
very impressive), turned to them with his toothy
smile, and said: "And now I'll tell you about a little
treat I've got in store for you. I'm going to do all
these tricks and a few more at this party of Ginger's
on Christmas Eve. I've been thinking over that party
and I'll tell you what I think we'll do. We'll have my
little conjuring show first, and then we'll have tea,
and then I'll tell them about my travels in Italy. You
remember you were much interested in them, Ginger,
old chap. I brought some slides of it down specially,
and we'll hire a magic lantern, and I think you'll find
that they'll all thoroughly enjoy it."

Ginger's mother was delighted with the suggestion.
She had been dreading Ginger's party. Her memories
of previous parties of Ginger's were nightmare memories

of Bedlam let loose.   She thought that Cousin Percy's
suggestion was an excellent one.   She couldn't understand Ginger's attitude to it.

"But, Ginger," she remonstrated, "I don't see what
you could have better.   Conjuring tricks and a magic
lantern.   It sounds ideal to me."

ON THE THIRD DAY OF HIS VISIT COUSIN PERCY BROUGHT
OUT HIS LITTLE CONJURING OUTFIT.

"Yes, but by *him*!" groaned Ginger. "Call them conjuring tricks! You can see him putting all the things in he takes out. An' the stuff he *talks*! An' lantern slides of the stuff he saw in It'ly! It's enough to make anyone sick."

"I simply can't understand you, Ginger," said Ginger's mother. "He's so charming and so good with boys. I'm sure that all the boys who come to the party will like him immensely."

But Ginger knew otherwise. And the Outlaws knew otherwise. From being a private thorn in their

THE OUTLAWS SAT IN A DEJECTED ROW, AND COUNTED THE MOMENTS TILL THE EXHIBITION SHOULD BE OVER.

flesh, Cousin Percy seemed likely to become a public humiliation. His smile, his voice, his breeziness, were so terribly mimicable. All the acquaintances and potential enemies who were to attend Ginger's party would have weapons of offence against them for years to come. The Outlaws had visions of a future in which their enemies pursued them through the village and over countryside with Cousin Percy's toothy smile and intolerable breeziness. "Now, you fellows . . ." "Now I'll tell you something that happened to me when I was just about your age." "Now, you fellows haven't any idea what I'm going to bring out of this hat. . . ."

And William's listlessness dropped from him. This calamity was not one to be meekly endured. It was one to be averted at all costs. . . .

Cousin Percy was pleased to see a new alertness in William as they took their daily walks abroad. William listened to him intently and watched him closely.

Cousin Percy said to Ginger's mother that evening: "I always notice that a boy smartens up when he's been with me for some time."

He could not know, of course, that William was watching him carefully for any weak spot that might be used against him. But Cousin Percy seemed to have very few weak spots.

The party was now only three days off, so that William had almost given up hope. Still, being William, he had not *quite* given up hope, and, as they walked along the road and Cousin Percy discoursed breezily and boisterously on the solar system, he was still watching him narrowly, listening to him intently. Cousin Percy, of course, thought that the interest was all for the solar system, and redoubled his breeziness.

"Yes, my boy, it's a wonderful thought that those dots that looks to us like the tiniest pinpricks in the heavens are really worlds as big as ours. Wonderful to think that——"

They were just turning into the lane that led back to Ginger's home. Suddenly Cousin Percy halted.

"It's a beautiful afternoon, boys, suppose we go back the longer way. If we hurry we shan't be late for tea."

Dejectedly the Outlaws turned with him to take the longer way. William, however, looked a little less dejected than a moment ago.

Right in the distance on the shorter road that Cousin Percy had decided not to take, William had caught sight of a herd of cows blocking the way. Cousin Percy, William concluded, had caught sight of them too.

The next day Cousin Percy went for a walk through the woods with the Outlaws to discuss the final arrangements for the party.

"I hope you haven't told your friends about me. It'll give Ginger a bit of a pull—what, old fellow?— when they find out that he's got a cousin who can do conjuring tricks. I remember well enough when I was about your age what a god a man seemed who could do conjuring tricks. Well, of course, it isn't everyone who can pick them up. It needs——"

"Excuse me," interrupted William, "I think that keeper wants to speak to me." And went off to a keeper who was walking through the undergrowth some distance away, and who certainly did not appear to have evinced any desire to speak to William.

He returned quickly. "He wanted to warn us that a mad bull's escaped from Jenks' farm an' got into the

wood. He says be very careful 'cause it's coming
this way. . . ."

Just near where they were standing was a small shed,
not much bigger than a dog-kennel, used by the keepers

COUSIN PERCY FLUNG HIMSELF IN WITH A CRY OF
TERROR, DREW THE DOOR TO, AND FASTENED IT.

to store food for the pheasants. It had a door and a
lock to protect it from marauders, but it was empty
now and the door hung open. Into this Cousin Percy
flung himself with a cry of terror, drew the door to,
and fastened it. It was a very tight fit but he just
managed it.

After a few seconds, however, he heard William's
reassuring voice:

"I say. It's all right. I made a mistake. He didn't say there was a mad bull. He said be sure and keep to the paths. I made a mistake."

Slowly, thoughtfully, Cousin Percy came out of his little shed. Slowly, thoughtfully, Cousin Percy accompanied them homewards. They made no reference to the incident, however, and he was recovering something of his breezy assurance by the time they reached Ginger's house. By the time they sat down to tea he had quite recovered it. But suddenly William raised his penetrating voice to address Ginger's mother:

"I made such a silly mistake to-day. We were in the wood an' I saw a keeper an' I thought he said there was a mad bull in the path an' I told Mr. Penshurst, an' he got into a little shed so as to be safe. We couldn't get into it, too, 'cause there was only room for Mr. Penshurst. An' then I found that I'd made a mistake, an' that what the keeper had really said was to be sure to keep to the paths. Wasn't it silly of me, makin' a mistake like that?"

Ginger's mother looked at Cousin Percy. Cousin Percy gulped and swallowed, and began to discuss the arrangements for the party. While he was discussing them, Henry's mother called to fetch him home, and to her, too, William told the story, resisting all Cousin Percy's attempts to guide the conversation into other channels.

"Wasn't it a silly mistake?" he said. "I mus' be goin' deaf. You see, I thought he said there was a mad bull in the wood, an' so Mr. Penshurst got into a little shed that there was jus' room for him in it an' we stayed outside, of course, 'cause there wasn't room for us in the little shed as well as Mr. Penhurst, an' then I

D

asked the keeper again what he'd said an' he said he'd only said 'mind an' keep on the paths.' Wasn't it silly of me makin' a mistake like that."

Cousin Percy, smiling a ghastly smile, said that, of course, he knew what the keeper had really said, and that he'd gone into the little shed to amuse the boys. But it wasn't convincing, and when William's mother came to ask Ginger's mother for her recipe for flapjacks and to take William home, and William went through the whole story again, he didn't even attempt the explanation. He merely smiled his ghastly smile.

"It's a jolly good joke against myself," said the suddenly voluble William, "and Mr. Penhurst said," with a polite nod in the direction of Cousin Percy, "that a manly boy ought to be the first to tell a joke against himself, so that's why I'm tellin' everyone about it. Fancy me bein' so silly as to think that he said there was a mad bull in the wood when all he said was to be sure to keep to the paths. An' givin' poor Mr. Penhurst the trouble of gettin' into that shed that was so little that there wasn't room for anyone else in it an' all 'cause I made such a silly mistake. I jolly well *deserve* to be laughed at about it."

Cousin Percy's smile grew yet ghastlier as he began to describe how he had once changed defeat into victory for his side at an important cricket match on his school's "playing fields."

But even Cousin Percy could see that his audience was distrait. They were listening to a description of Cousin Percy turning defeat into victory for his side on his school's "playing fields," but they were thinking of Cousin Percy fastening himself safely into the little shed leaving William, Ginger, Henry and Douglas outside. . . .

The next day was the day before the party. William, Henry and Douglas went as usual to call for Ginger and Cousin Percy, and they all set off for a walk.

Cousin Percy was his most breezy and boisterous. He evidently meant to start afresh, and to blot out completely the memory of yesterday's unfortunate incident. But William didn't. William told the story to everyone they met in the village, told it with a sort of deprecating modesty as a proof of his own stupidity.

"I keep rememb'rin' what you said about a manly boy bein' the first to tell a joke about himself," he remarked again guilelessly to Cousin Percy, "that's why I'm tellin' them all."

And even when Cousin Percy informed him rather sharply that it was not necessary to carry it to extremes, he still continued to relate the story to all he met.

Cousin Percy endured it till tea-time, when William dropped his final bombshell.

"I bet all the boys at the party to-morrow will laugh at me," he said, "when I tell 'em of the silly mistake I made yesterday."

It was then that Cousin Percy told Ginger's mother that he was sorry not to be able to stay over Christmas after all, but that urgent business would take him home first thing to-morrow morning. He added that he was sorry to miss Ginger's party.

Ginger's mother retained a pathetic trust in him in spite of everything. As the fun of Ginger's party waxed fast and furious, and one crowd of boys pursued another crowd of boys with ear-splitting war whoops up the front stairs and down the back, Ginger's mother wrung her hands and said plaintively to William's mother:

"If only Cousin Percy hadn't had to go home, they'd *never* have got as rowdy as this! He's so wonderful with boys."

CHAPTER V

WILLIAM AND THE TEMPORARY HISTORY MASTER

WILLIAM had thought that school could not possibly be worse than it was, but quite suddenly—half-way through the term—he discovered his mistake. The history master, a mild and elderly man, conveniently short-sighted, conveniently deaf, and still more conveniently fond of expounding his own historical theories without in the least minding whether anyone listened to them or not, caught scarlet fever and was removed to hospital.

For a few glorious lessons William's form spent the history hour officially doing homework, but in reality indulging in such sports and pastimes as dart-throwing, earwig racing, ruler-and-rubber cricket, and ink slinging. Then the "temporary" arrived—a small, smug man with protruding teeth and a manner that hovered between the hearty, the jocular, and the sarcastic. He had, moreover, modern theories about the teaching of history. He believed in making it real by acting it. When he gave a lesson on the Magna Charta one of the boys had to be King John and the others the turbulent barons. When he gave a lesson on Charles I, one of them had to be Charles I, and another the executioner, and so on. The novelty of this proceeding had long worn off as far as Mr. Renies himself was concerned, and he now relieved the monot-

ony of it as far as possible by choosing for the principal
and most dramatic parts boys who were obviously
devoid of histrionic talent. This enabled him to make
clever little jibes at their clumsiness, jibes that were
always rewarded by the sycophantic titters of the other
boys. Mr. Renies loved these sycophantic titters. He
didn't consider them sycophantic, of course. He
considered them honest tributes to his sparkling wit
and brilliant flashes of humour. Mr. Renies, it is
perhaps unnecessary to add, thought a great deal of
himself, more in fact than most other people thought of
him. He was certainly clever in picking out the right
boy for his butt—self-conscious, inarticulate, and yet
not insensitive.

On the first day on which Mr. Renies faced William's
form he looked round for his butt and his eye fell on
William. William, it must be admitted, looked the
part to perfection.

"What's your name?" said Mr. Renies.

"Brown," admitted William suspiciously.

Mr. Renies' face beamed with anticipatory pleasure.

"Well, Brown," he said kindly, "suppose you come
out here and give us your idea of Charles the First
before the House of Commons demanding the arrest of
the five members . . ."

Alone or with his Outlaws William could act the
hero in the most stirring scenes that the imagination
could possibly conceive, but to be ordered to act
as part of a lesson by this objectionable little man
was quite another thing. Reluctantly he came up to
the front of the class. There he stood, purple-faced
with anger and embarrassment, glaring ferociously at
Mr. Renies and the class. Mr. Renies' smile broadened.
He enlivened the lesson with frequent references to

"this kingly figure" . . . "this mien of majesty," and
was rewarded as usual by a chorus of titters from boys
who were relieved that his choice had fallen on William
and not on them.

The next day he ordered William to impersonate

RELUCTANTLY WILLIAM CAME UP TO THE FRONT OF THE
CLASS. THERE HE STOOD, PURPLE WITH ANGER AND
EMBARRASSMENT, GLARING FEROCIOUSLY AT THE MASTER.

Prince Rupert and the day after that Oliver Cromwell.
William impersonated both by the simple means of
staring furiously and doggedly in front of him, and
Mr. Renies' enjoyment increased.

He referred to him as "this noble youth," "this

valiant hero," and even as "this spirited young
actor."

William disliked it, but saw no other course than to
endure it. He had no weapon against Mr. Renies
except in his imagination, and he worked his imagination very hard during those days. There had been a
side show in the last fair that had visited the village
called "Picture of 200 different forms of Torture," and
William had paid his 1*d*. entrance fee and spent an
enthralled half-hour in the tent. He now put Mr.
Renies in imagination through every one of the two
hundred forms of torture. As Mr. Renies, gay and
debonair, stood at his desk and poured forth his stream
of little witticisms, he had no idea of course that
William saw him writhing on a rack or struggling in
boiling oil. In fact so horrible and so real were these
pictures to William that he couldn't help feeling that
he had scored. After all, what was being made to feel
a fool before the class in comparison with being im-
paled on spikes and rolled down-hill in a barrel full of
nails—things that happened to Mr. Renies several
times an hour? But even Mr. Renies could go too
far.

"Now, Brown," he said, with his toothy smile, "we
must think out a nice part for you for next revision
lesson. How about—he rose to dazzling heights of
wit—making you Henrietta Maria and I'll be Bucking-
ham and come to woo you? That would be nice,
boys, wouldn't it?" The bored titter that Mr.
Renies looked upon as a spontaneous tribute to his
wit broke out again dutifully, and Mr. Renies continued:
"Our young actor doesn't look pleased. . . . You
must come round to my house some evening, my friend,
and we'll practise some of these rôles together."

William began to be dimly aware that this state of things could not go on, and that something must be done about it, but it was a quite justifiable action on the part of Mr. Renies that finally roused him.

Mr. Renies was in the habit of confiscating any article with which he saw his pupils playing, and, finding William opening the back of his watch and trying to replace a little wheel that he had taken out to sharpen a pencil point, he confiscated it. The watch had not been going for some weeks, and in any case William never cared what time it was, so it cannot be said that the loss of the watch as a means of telling the time seriously inconvenienced him. In fact, if his mother had not had a letter from the aunt who had given him the watch, saying that she was coming to see them the next week and adding facetiously that she need not bring her grandfather clock because William would be able to tell her the time by his nice new watch, William would never have thought of it again. The fact that the watch wasn't going wouldn't matter, of course. His aunt, aware that it was a cheap watch and unaware that William took from it regularly any of its component parts that he needed for his various experiments (such as making a motor-launch, or a treadwheel for his pet stag beetle), would merely have offered to pay for it being mended, as she had already done once or twice. But the fact that it had passed out of his possession entirely would matter a great deal. Aunts are notoriously touchy on such points, and it would probably matter so much that she would not give him the customary tip on her departure. Therefore William decided by hook or by crook to recover his watch. He gave Mr. Renies the chance of acting magnanimously by asking for it. He asked for it when

Mr. Renies was alone in the form-room, and, as there was no appreciative audience to render him its homage of titters, Mr. Renies wasted none of his famous wit on William, but merely snapped "Certainly not!"

Therefore no course was left to William, as William saw the situation, but that of entering Mr. Renies' house, where presumably Mr. Renies kept his ill-gotten gains, and taking the watch from Mr. Renies as lawlessly as, William considered, Mr. Renies had taken it from him.

And so the night before his aunt's visit William approached the history master's house (where Mr. Renies was temporarily domiciled), having left Mr. Renies in his form-room correcting exercises.

He knocked boldly at the front door. A maid wearing a grimy apron and a dreamy expression came to answer his knock.

"I've called with a message from Mr. Renies," said William, meeting her eye squarely, "he says you needn't stop in any longer this evening. You can go out now."

The maid, fortunately for William, was of a simple and credulous disposition. Moreover she was in love. To go out meant meeting the beloved, therefore she was willing to believe implicitly any message that told her to go out.

"What about his supper?" she said.

"Oh, he won't be a minute," said William reassuringly. "He says just leave it ready."

"What about locking up?" said the maid, who was already in imagination walking down a country lane clasped tightly in the stalwart arm of the beloved.

"He says put the key on the window-sill," said William.

A few minutes later the maid laid the key upon the window-sill and flew on winged feet to Paradise and the beloved.

A few minutes later still William took the key from the window-sill and opened the front door.

*   *   *   *   *

Mr. Renies walked slowly up to his house. He felt pleased with the world in general and himself in particular. He had finished his corrections early, he had got some good fun out of that kid—what was his name—Brown—he was going home to a delicious supper of pheasant, bread sauce, baked potatoes, brussels sprouts, followed by a pineapple cream and a savoury. Mr. Renies liked to do himself well, but it wasn't often that he could rise to such heights as this. The supper was in honour of the pheasant that had been sent to him by a cousin who was staying at a "shoot." Mr. Renies had been looking forward to it all day.

He opened his front door and stood for a minute in the hall, dilating his nostrils and drawing in the delicious odour with an anticipatory smile. Then he hung up his hat, washed his hands, called out: "I'm ready, Ellen," and went toward the dining-room, rubbing his hands, and smacking his lips. He flung open the door and entered. And there the first shock awaited him. Upon the table stood a dish containing the well-picked carcase of a pheasant, flanked by empty vegetable dishes. At his place was an empty well-scraped plate that had recently contained pheasant, bread sauce, baked potatoes, gravy and brussels sprouts. On it were laid at an unconventional angle the knife and fork that had evidently been used in the consumption of the repast.

There was an empty dish that had evidently once contained a pineapple cream and another dish that had evidently contained a savoury. For a moment Mr. Renies was literally paralysed with horror and amazement. His eyes grew fixed and glassy. His mouth dropped open. Then he cried: "Ellen!" and rushed to the kitchen. The kitchen was empty. Ellen's cap and apron were hung neatly behind the door. He called: "Ellen!" still more wildly, but no one answered. It was quite clear that Ellen was no longer in the house. Mr. Renies dashed upstairs to his study. And there the second shock awaited him. The drawer in which he kept the articles that he confiscated in school was open and empty.

"Burglars!" was his first thought but he found on examination that nothing else in the room was missing. Then he heard a sound in the big cupboard by the window, and for a moment the wild idea flashed into his head that rats were responsible for everything—the eating of his supper, the emptying of the drawers and the strange noise in the cupboard. He remembered in time, however, that rats do not use knives and forks. He flung open the cupboard door and there he got his third shock. For William crouched in the cupboard blinking at him.

William had not really meant to eat Mr. Renies' supper. He had peeped into the dining-room and found the meal laid there. It looked very appetising, and William was very hungry. William decided to eat a very little of it, so little that Mr. Renies couldn't possibly notice. It wasn't till he discovered that he had eaten so much that Mr. Renies couldn't possibly help noticing it, that he decided that he might as well finish it. So he finished it and thoroughly enjoyed it. It was, he decided, the best meal he'd ever had in his life (better even than Christmas dinner because there was no one there to worry him about manners), and worth any consequences. Then he went upstairs to find his watch. He found it quite easily in the first drawer he opened. With it were a penknife of Ginger's, a mouth organ of Douglas's, a catapult of Henry's and numerous other articles belonging to other boys. William decided that he might as well take them all. He would give their property back to Ginger and Henry and Douglas and sell the rest to their owners. William possessed a strong commercial instinct. Just as he was putting the last article (a pistol belonging to Smith minimus) into his pocket he heard someone enter the house. He stood still and listened. Soon there came a ferocious bellow, angry cries of "Ellen!" and the sound of heavy footsteps ascending the stairs. Without a moment's hesitation William flung himself into the only cupboard the room possessed and closed the doors. Unfortunately the cupboard was already full of other things than William, and William's figure, though small, was not the sort of figure to accommodate itself to the thin zig-zag line of space left between a pile of books, a duplicating machine, half a dozen croquet mallets, a dozen Indian clubs, an old-fashioned camera on a stand and a large moth-eaten stag's head with branching antlers. With great difficulty he took up a posture that was in the shape of the letter S, but one of the stag's antlers was digging so mercilessly into his neck that he moved slightly in order to relieve the pressure, and knocked over the pile of books. Almost immediately the cupboard door was flung open, and the amazed and furious face of Mr. Renies appeared. William was glad to be saved from the murderous attack of the moth-eaten stag, but otherwise he realised that the situation was a delicate one. There was no doubt at all that Mr. Renies was very angry. He dragged William out by his ear and thundered:

"WHAT IS THE MEANING OF THIS?" THUNDERED MR. RENIES.

"What is the meaning of this?"

For a moment William was at a loss how to answer, then inspiration came to him. He assumed a vacant expression.

"Please, sir," he said, "you asked me to come to your house an' practise actin' history scenes some

"PLEASE, SIR," REPLIED WILLIAM, "YOU ASKED ME TO COME TO YOUR HOUSE AND PRACTISE ACTING HISTORY SCENES."

evening, so I came, an' I was jus' practis'n' bein'
Charles the First in hidin' when you came in."

Mr. Renies sputtered angrily. His eye fell upon the
empty drawer.

"And did you *dare*," he stormed, "to open a private
drawer of mine and empty it?"

Inspiration again came to William. He realised
with surprise that he knew more history than he had
thought.

"No, sir," he said innocently, "I was practisin'
being Jack Cade's rebellion lootin' and plunderin'."

Then the memory of the supreme outrage of that
evening came back to Mr. Renies, and for a minute his
fury and anguish deprived him of the power of speech.
Finally he stuttered:

"And—and—and—downstairs—was it *you* who
dared to——"

William by now had his wits well about him.

"That?" he said. "Oh yes, sir. I was practisin'
actin' that king that died of a surfeit of lampreys. I
couldn't find any lampreys so I jus' had to eat what I
could find. I didn't die of it either but that wasn't
my fault."

With a howl of fury Mr. Renies flung himself
upon William, but William was already half-way
downstairs.

"I'm practisin' bein' Charles II fleein' after the
battle of Worcester," he called over his shoulder as he
ran.

Mr. Renies plunged downstairs after him. This
was an occasion for immediate revenge. A man as
deeply outraged in his dignity and his stomach as Mr.
Renies had been does not defer punishment till the
next morning. The pleasant perfume of roast pheasant

that hung about the hall increased his anger to the point of madness as he passed through it. In the dusk he could see the figure of William fleeing down the road. He followed, and fury lent wings to him. Fury, in fact, lent such wings that William began to feel slightly disconcerted. It is not easy to run really fast on such a meal as William had just partaken of, and there was no doubt that Mr. Renies was gaining on him. That retribution must follow the evening's exploit sooner or later William was well aware, but he preferred it to be later rather than sooner. Certainly he didn't want to receive it at the hands of an enraged Mr. Renies in the middle of the road. Mr. Renies was a better runner than he looked, and slowly but steadily he was gaining on his quarry. It was too late now even to plunge through the hedge into a field. The time it would take to turn off from the road would deliver him into his enemy's hands. And William rightly judged that it would take more than a hedge to stop the raging pheasantless man behind him. He was quite near him now. Almost upon him. Only a miracle could save William. Turning a sharp bend in the road he ran into his sister, who was taking a leisurely walk with a girl friend. Nimbly William dodged aside and took cover behind them. Round the corner immediately after him came Mr. Renies, his arms outstretched to catch that little fiend who was at last within his grasp. He collided violently with Ethel and her friend. He lost his balance and clung to them to save himself—an arm round the neck of each. From behind them came William's voice breathless but quite distinct.

"This is Mr. Renies, Ethel," he said. "He's our history master. He goes about actin' history scenes.

He's actin'" . . . the sight of Mr. Renies, still clasping
the necks of Ethel and her friend in an attempt to
recover his balance suggested, an irresistible parallel—
"he's actin' he's Henry the Eighth now," he ended
and disappeared into the dusk.

NIMBLY WILLIAM DODGED ASIDE AND TOOK COVER
BEHIND HIS SISTER AND HER FRIEND.

He didn't disappear alone, however. Mr. Renies, his fury again roused to boiling-point, dashed after him. William had had a slight start, but the added fury of Mr. Renies' spirit again seemed to give speed to his feet. Again he was on the point of catching William, when William suddenly darted through the open garden gate belonging to a house that bordered the road.

ROUND THE CORNER CAME MR. RENIES, HIS ARMS OUT-
STRETCHED TO CATCH THAT LITTLE FIEND WHO WAS AT
LAST WITHIN HIS GRASP.

William knew the garden well. There was a lily pond in the middle of the lawn. William sometimes took a forbidden short cut through the garden and took the lily pond literally in his stride. He cleared it now with a skill born of long practise. Mr. Renies was at a disadvantage. He didn't know that there was a lily pond and in the dusk he did not notice it. He followed William's flying figure and—found himself up to the shoulders in water. The sound of the splash and of the shout of anger and surprise that accompanied it, brought an elderly lady down from the house to investigate. She found a man floundering in her lily pond and a boy standing by the side watching him.

"What on earth does this mean?" asked the lady majestically.

Mr. Renies tried to explain, but he couldn't, because he'd swallowed a pint of water and several lily buds in his sudden descent.

"Is he drunk?" went on the lady.

"No," said William, "he's not exactly drunk. He's Mr. Renies, our history master. He goes about acting history scenes. He's acting now that this is the sea, that he's the king's son that was drowned in the sea and never smiled again."

"He must be *mad*," said the lady indignantly.

Mr. Renies again made frenzied efforts to explain, but all he could do was to spit out lily buds.

"He's not exactly mad," said William indulgently, "He's just got this craze for actin' history scenes. I go about with him to see he doesn't do too much damage."

"But he's *ruining* the lily pond," said the lady.

"I know," said William sadly, "but he *would* go

into it. When he thinks of a scene he wants to act nothin' can stop him."

The lady turned to Mr. Renies indignantly.

"You ought to be ashamed of yourself," she said, "get out of my pond at once or I'll send for the police."

William had discreetly vanished into the dusk.

"Listen!" sputtered Mr. Renies wildly, but the lady had turned on her heel and gone into the house, whither she sent a man servant to expel Mr. Renies from the pond and to inform him that if he wasn't out of the garden within five minutes she was going to send for the police.

Dripping and dishevelled, Mr. Renies stumbled out of the garden gate into the road. He peered about him, but there was no sign of William. Then from above his head came a small distinct voice.

"I'm actin' being Charles II in the oak tree now . . ."

Mr. Renies ignored it. Wet, cold and hungry he staggered homewards.

*   *   *   *   *

Mr. Renies' first thought was to lay the whole matter before the headmaster. For a boy to go to a master's house, eat his supper, ransack his drawers, hide in his cupboard, then lead him a dance over the countryside, was surely a crime unknown before in the annals of school life. Then Mr. Renies began to wonder whether it would be really wise to lay the whole matter before the headmaster. The episodes that took place in his house were all right. It was the episodes that took place outside his house that made him hesitate. He saw himself clinging to those two girls, he saw himself floundering in the lily pond. . . . Of course, he needn't mention those episodes, but he was beginning to know William a little better, and he was afraid that William's conscience would lead him to "confess" them. He saw himself the laughing-stock of the village. As things were, that might be avoided. He had heard one of the two girls say crossly: "That *awful* boy." Obviously they knew William and felt only annoyance with him. He could go to see the lady of the lily pond, and make up some story that would satisfy her. (He could say that he thought the boy had fallen into the lily pond and had plunged in to rescue him.) There wasn't any reason why anyone else should know anything about it. William might tell? Mr. Renies had a shrewd idea that, properly treated, William would not tell. . . .

He changed from his wet clothes and sat down to write to his cousin thanking him for the pheasant. He said with bitterness in his heart that it had been delicious. A funny thing about that boy, he reflected as he stamped and addressed the letter. He'd thought him a perfectly safe butt for his little jokes. One did sometimes make mistakes however. . . .

The next morning Mr. Renies entered the class-room, sat down at the master's desk, and said: "Open your note-books, please."

"Please, sir, aren't we going to have any acting to-day?" said a boy in the front row.

"Acting?" repeated Mr. Renies, as if he did not understand.

"Yes, sir. Acting history scenes."

"Acting history scenes?" said Mr. Renies in a tone of great surprise and indignation, "of course not. I never heard of such a thing. Open your note-books and take down the following dates." Then politely, almost affectionately, in the tone in which a master speaks to a favourite pupil, he added: "Would you mind cleaning the board for me, please, Brown?"

A close observer would have noticed a rather peculiar smile on William's face, as he rose obediently from his desk and began to clean the board.

CHAPTER VI

A CROWDED HOUR WITH WILLIAM

WILLIAM'S mother was making cakes at the kitchen table, and William was watching the operation with melancholy interest.

"I can't think what you *do* it for," he said.

"Do what for, dear?" she asked absently.

"Cook it," said William, "it's much nicer before you start cooking it," and added bitterly, "not that I've ever had enough to taste hardly."

"But you always scrape out the dish, dear," protested his mother. "I'm going to let you scrape out the dish now. And the spoon."

William laughed sardonically.

"Huh! An' there's likely to be a lot on, isn't there?" he said. "Anyone'd think you were tryin' to *starve* me the way you scrape it out."

"But you've had a very good breakfast," his mother reminded him.

"Breakfast!" ejaculated William with infinite contempt.

She began to scrape out the cake mixture and put it into little tins. William watched her with agonised eyes and ejaculations of incredulous surprise.

"Gosh! Fancy scrapin' it out like *that*! Crumbs! You'll have the basin in *bits* soon, scrapin' it like that. It must be a jolly strong basin. Why, you've not left enough to *see*. A *fly* wouldn't bother to eat what you've left. A——"

"Now, William," his mother interrupted him firmly, "I've left quite a lot. If you don't want it, of course, you needn't have it. I'll put the basin to soak in the sink."

But William, who had been talking for talking's sake and because he considered that to admit that a reasonable amount of cake mixture had been left in the dish might prejudice his chance of getting more next time, hastily seized it and set to work upon it earnestly.

"It's jolly good," he said as he emerged from the final stage of the ceremony that left the dish as clean as if it had been washed.

"Oh *William*," sighed his mother, "you've got it on your hair *and* your ears."

"Where?" said William as if interested to hear that traces of the delicious mixture was still in existence.

"Go and wash, William," commanded his mother sternly.

William went to wash and returned to find his mother closing the oven door, having deposited the tray of cakes inside.

"Jus' let me eat *one* of 'em raw," he said, "then I promise I won't eat any of the others cooked. I'd rather have one raw than hundreds cooked."

"No, William," said his mother, "they're not for you in any case. They're for the Women's Guild Exhibition."

"The Women's Guild?" repeated William in indignant horror. "What're *they* wantin' our cakes for?"

"It's a competition for home-made things,"

explained Mrs. Brown patiently, "and I'm entering for the cakes. There's cakes and jam and bottled fruits and wine and pickles and things like that."

"What do you get for a prize?" said William.

"A badge."

"A *what*?"

"A badge."

"*Crumbs!*" said William. "Nothin' more than that?"

"No. It's the honour and glory that counts."

"I'd rather have cakes than honour and glory any day," said William simply. "What happens to the cakes?"

"They go to the Cottage Hospital for the sick people."

"Gosh!" said William. "Cakes like that *wasted* on sick people! Well, I've been sick, so I *know*. I think it's *unkind* to send 'em to sick people. Tell you what——"

But William's mother cut him short.

"Now, William, don't stay in here chattering. I'm busy. You can help me carry the cakes down to the Village Hall after tea if you like."

William greeted this suggestion with an ironic laugh.

"Huh! Thanks. It's *jolly* kind of you to let me carry down cakes that I'm not allowed to eat and that are going to be used makin' sick people worse. *Jolly* kind!"

But still William never liked to be out of anything that was going on, and after tea he appeared as if by accident as his mother was just setting off with her basket.

"I jus' happen to be goin' down to the village," he said casually, "so I'll come along with you."

She refused his offer to carry the basket and they set off together to the Village Hall.

There William watched the scene with amazed interest. Crowds of women were placing dishes of cakes, jars of jam or pickles, on long trestle tables, behind which stood other women wearing blue overalls and expressions that became more and more apprehensive as they surveyed the growing array of products that would have to be judged.

"My dear," murmured one to the other, "I had indigestion for *months* after it last year, and there seems to be even more this."

William overheard this remark and was encouraged by it to approach his mother with an offer that he made in a hoarse whisper.

"I don't mind helpin' judge the cakes," he said. "I mean I'll taste 'em an' tell the people what they taste like, then it'll save 'em the trouble of tastin' 'em. I'm only thinkin' of savin' them trouble. . . ."

"Of course not, William," said his mother firmly.

She had put the cakes on a plate on the trestle table and by it a card bearing her name and address. William looked at the cakes. They were small but very delicious-looking, the top of each decorated by a preserved cherry. William adored preserved cherries.

"May I have jus' *one* for helping you bring them?"

"No, William, of course not," said his mother, "and you didn't help bring them."

William had recourse to his sardonic laugh again.

"Huh! *Well*," he said, gazing about the room, "seems funny to me to make all this stuff just for badges an' people that would sooner be without it. I 'spect it'll *kill* someone at the Cottage Hospital an' then you'll all get into trouble an'," darkly, "don't say I didn't warn you."

His mother promised that she wouldn't, and they set off homeward with the empty basket.

The next morning William had completely forgotten the competition in the Village Hall. It was Saturday, and he rose gaily to a day of glorious freedom.

He spent the morning in the woods playing Red Indians with his Outlaws, but in the afternoon time began to hang heavily on his hands. Ginger had reluctantly gone under escort to pay a visit to his dentist; Douglas, also reluctantly, was staying at home to receive a visit from his godmother; and Henry had been forbidden to come out owing to the state in which he had arrived home after the morning's Red Indian game, in the process of which he had rolled into a stream with William, and, unfortunately for him, William had happened to be on top.

William therefore was left to his own devices. He didn't feel in the mood for his own devices and wandered aimlessly down the road hoping to meet a kindred spirit. The spirit he met, however, was far from being a kindred one. It was the spirit of Hubert Lane, who had been the bitter foe of the Outlaws from time, to the Outlaws, immemorial. Or rather it was the body of Hubert Lane, for Hubert Lane was fat and sly and possessed much discretion but very little spirit. The feud between Hubert Lane and the Outlaws happened to be passing through a quiescent period, so William merely passed Hubert with a hostile grimace. At least William tried to pass Hubert with a hostile grimace. But the grimace, beginning splendidly as a hideous facial contortion expressive of hatred and defiance, faded away, despite all William's

endeavours, into a sheepish grin. For Hubert Lane
was not alone. He was accompanied by a little girl of
about his own age, but of very different appearance—a
little girl with dark eyes, dark curly hair, and smooth
dimpled cheeks. An indisputably attractive little
girl. A little girl of whom he was obviously unworthy
to be the companion. William slackened his pace.
The little girl slackened hers.

"Ask that boy," William heard her say to
Hubert.

"Him!" said Hubert with a scorn that brought the
lust of battle to William's heart, "not likely."

"But why not, Hubert?" persisted the little girl.
"He might know. He might have a watch. And it's
silly not knowing the time."

"I'm not going to ask *him*," said Hubert again in
a tone that inflamed still further the lust of battle in
William's heart.

"I will, then," said the little girl. She turned
suddenly and came towards William, who was standing
in the middle of the road, wholly absorbed apparently
in the contemplation of the horizon.

"Please, boy," she said distantly, "could you tell
us the time? Hubert came out without his watch and
I've not got one yet. I'm going to have one when I'm
twelve."

William looked at her as if realising her presence
with a start.

"I beg your pardon," he said with excessive
politeness, "I din' see you. I was jus' thinkin'
about somethin'." He said this in order that she
should not suspect that he had stopped in order to
look after her. "I often do that," he went on garru-
lously, "stand an' think a bit in the road."

But the little girl was not interested in William's power of thought.

"Can you tell us the time, please?" she said impatiently.

"Oh yes," said William, determined to prolong the conversation to its utmost limits. "Yes, I c'n tell you the time all right." He felt leisurely in his jacket pocket. "Got my watch here, all right, I expect. . . . No, it doesn't seem to be here. I expect it's in the other pocket." He felt exhaustively in the other pocket. "What's your name?" he said conversationally as he searched.

"Dorinda," said the little girl still impatiently.

"Mine's William," volunteered William.

She betrayed no interest in this fact—only said shortly:

"Isn't your watch in that pocket?"

"No, it doesn't seem to be," said William in a tone of great surprise. "Funny thing it not bein' in either of these pockets. I 'spect it's in my trouser pocket."

He began a lengthy search in a trouser pocket, saying meanwhile:

"Where do you live?"

"In Godalming," said the little girl. "I'm Hubert's cousin, and I've come to spend the day with them."

It was evident that she did not offer this information with any idea of reciprocating William's friendly overtures. She spoke curtly, her frowning gaze fixed on the spot where William's hand was still engaged in its shameless search for a non-existent watch.

"It *can't* be in that pocket," she went on with distinct annoyance in her tone, "if you haven't found it yet."

"No," agreed William confidingly, "I was jus'

beginnin' to think it couldn't. I'll have a look in the other. How long are you staying?"

"Only to-day. Well, it can't be in that one either, can it?"

"I 'spose not," agreed William reluctantly, "but I thought I might have a good look while I was about it. There's my waistcoat pockets yet, I'll have a good look in all of those now."

But the little girl had lightly slipped her fingers one after the other into his waistcoat pockets before he had realised what she was doing.

"It's not in those either," she said.

"I must have lost it," said William trying to assume the anguished expression of one who has just discovered the loss of a valuable watch. "It mus' have dropped out of my pocket on to the road as I came along. Tell you what, I'll walk back with you 'n' try 'n' find it."

Delighted with the ruse, he set off with the little girl towards Hubert, who stood several yards away from them with an expression of patient aloofness on his fat and pallid countenance.

"He's lost his watch, Hubert," she explained. "He thinks he must have dropped it somewhere on the road. He's coming back with us to find out."

Hubert turned his small malignant eyes upon William.

"He's not got a watch," he said.

William temporised as best he could in the face of this undoubted truth.

"Huh!" he said, "a lot you know about it."

"I know you've not got one."

"Oh, do you," said William sarcastically. "Well, you know a bit too much. Let *me* tell *you* my aunt gave me one for Christmas."

"Yes, and you tried to make a bomb out of it last week with some gunpowder, and a lot of things in your house got blown up, and there wasn't any of the watch left at all, and your father said you'd not to have another till you were twenty-one even if anyone gave you one."

"Whoever told you a silly tale like that?" said William, but he spoke feebly, knowing that to Hubert's companion the story must bear the stamp of truth.

"I'll prove it to you," said Hubert in his most superior tone. "Our cook's your cook's sister an' she was in your house when it happened. An' she said you got into a jolly row—so there!"

"She was makin' it up, pullin' your leg," said William, but he spoke without any serious hope of convincing either of them.

They had been walking slowly and had just come to a bend in the road.

"There's the church clock," cried Dorinda suddenly, "so it's all right, and it doesn't matter about his watch." She addressed William with haughty politeness. "Good-bye, an' I'm sorry we troubled you."

"Oh, *that's* all right," said William effusively, "that's quite all right. It wasn't any trouble at all. Not at all. I *like* takin' trouble for people. Well, I happen to be goin' this way so I'll walk along with you, shall I?"

Their silence quite obviously did not give consent, but William was of tougher metal than to be quelled by a snub. He joined them, walking on the other side of Dorinda, and raised his voice pleasantly in conversation.

"I can tell you some jolly interestin' things," he

said. "I can tell you lots of things you don't know about Red Indians and pirates and smugglers and stag-beetles and wasps and caterpillars and huntin' wild beasts and things like that."

They ignored him. Dorinda presented the back of her head to him, turning her face to Hubert.

"*Do* go on, Hubert," she said enthusiastically. "Tell me more about that place you went to last holidays."

"Munich?" drawled Hubert loftily. "It's in Germany, you know. I picked up quite a lot of German there."

"I could tell you things I've done you'd hardly believe," announced William. "Fightin' Red Indians an' catchin' pirates an' things like that."

In his imaginary adventures William identified himself sometimes with the Red Indians and pirates and sometimes with their attackers. Whichever side he led, of course, conquered. But the little girl took no notice of him. Her head remained turned away from him to Hubert.

"Tell me more about Munich, Hubert," she pleaded.

"We went to see art galleries and museums and things," said Hubert, "and"—his small eyes suddenly glistening—"we stayed at a hotel where they gave us jolly decent food."

There was, as William saw it, only one thing to do and he did it. He stepped back, then suddenly inserted himself between Hubert and Dorinda, so that Dorinda's eager smiling face was turned to him.

"I can tell you some jolly interesting things about smugglers, too," he said.

But Hubert, after an ineffectual attempt to push

E

him back, had gone round to Dorinda's other side, and Dorinda at once turned to him, presenting to William again a cold quarter profile.

"Tell me some things you saw there, Hubert."

"Oh, I saw a lot of things," said Hubert grandly, "statues and things."

"What sort of statues?"

William tried to repeat the ruse, but Hubert was prepared for it and braced his stout body to resist the passage of William's between him and Dorinda.

"Oh, kings and people," said Hubert, digging an elbow hard into William's stomach, "and there's a sort of palace where a sort of king used to live and a big bridge with a river underneath and——"

His voice died away. After the attack on his stomach William had fallen back, but he was now walking on Hubert's heels, and Hubert despite himself was beginning to hurry.

He still talked to Dorinda, but somewhat disconnectedly.

"And—there's—a sort—of—garden. Ow!"

"Why are you walking so fast, Hubert?"

"I'm not. It's—*Ow!*"

Suddenly it was William who was next to her.

"What sort of books do you like best?" said William. William had realised with reluctance that she was not interested in pirates and smugglers and had decided to try another subject. He had, while spending a day in bed with a cold last month, read a book whose plot he meant to recount to her—a plot of hauntings and murders and arch criminals and fights in the dark and wild pursuits over land and sea, a plot in fact after his own heart.

She was taken aback by William's sudden appearance

and had answered his question before she had realised that it was he who had put it.

"Fairy tales," she said, then turned at once to Hubert who had betaken himself to her other side. "What sort of a garden, Hubert?"

"Oh—a sort of—a garden just like an English garden," said Hubert.

"I'm jolly good at magic myself," said William modestly. That arrested her. She turned to him slowly.

"You can't be," she said, "only magicians are good at magic."

"Well, I'm a magician," said William. His tone of finality and certitude was rather impressive. Dorinda looked at him incredulous, but interested.

"You!" she said.

"He's not a magician," said Hubert. "I can tell you that."

"Oh, aren't I?" said William meaningly.

"Well, you tell me one bit of magic you've ever done," challenged Hubert.

"I made a trifle and some cakes come out of nothing in a cupboard at a party of yours," said William.

He referred to a dramatic occasion when, having looked through the window and seen Hubert hiding the trifle and cakes before his party so that he and his cronies could consume them alone afterwards, he had concealed his knowledge till the middle of tea, then pretended to produce them from their hiding-place by magic.

Hubert sheered away quickly from this reference.

"Oh that!" he said, "that was nothing. You're no more a magician than I am."

"All right, do something then if *you're* a magician. Turn something into something."

"I'd do it as well as you could, anyway."

"All right.   Do it."

"*Both* turn something into something," said Dorinda excitedly.   "Hubert, do it first."

"Well, I bet I can do anything he can," said Hubert,

"I'M AFRAID IT'S MAGIC FOOD," SAID WILLIAM.   "YOU CAN'T EAT IT."

"it was him that said he was a magician.   I only said I was as much one as he was considering he wasn't one at all."

But Dorinda was thrilled by the idea and refused to abandon it.

"Both *try* to do magic, anyway," she said.   "I tell

you what, I'm frightfully hungry, and in the fairy tale I was reading last night, when the princess began to get frightfully hungry, the magician commanded a large

BUT THE LITTLE GIRL WAS ALREADY AT THE TABLE.
"I CAN EAT IT," SHE SAID.

room full of food to appear, and it did.   You do that, Hubert.   Say 'I command a large room full of food to appear,' and see if it does."

"I command a large room full of food to appear," said Hubert, and added impatiently: "Of course it won't.   I knew it wouldn't."

Dorinda had to admit rather regretfully that it hadn't.

"Now let William try," she said.

"Yes," sneered Hubert, "let William try an' see if he does it any better. It's him that said he was a magician."

An idea had come to William. "I can't do it jus' this minute," he said. "I'll do it when I get jus' by that lamppost. My magic's always strongest when I'm near a lamppost."

They walked to the lamppost, Dorinda watching him eagerly, Hubert sniggering.

He stood by the lamppost opposite the door of the Village Hall and said: "I command a big room full of food to appear."

Then he flung open the door of the Village Hall.

In a large room empty of human beings stood trestle tables laden with cakes and jam and bottled fruits and other delicacies. Hubert's eyes protruded in amazement. Hubert's mother had no dealings with the Women's Guild and he had heard nothing of the Cookery Exhibition in the Village Hall. The little girl clasped her hands and gasped.

"Oh; how wonderful!"

Triumph filled William's heart, then slowly ebbed away leaving apprehension.

"I'm afraid it's magic food," he said to the little girl, "you can't axshully *eat* it. There's a spell laid on it that my magic's not strong enough to take off."

But the little girl was already at the cake table munching energetically.

"But it *is*, William," she said indistinctly, "it *has* taken it off. I *can* eat it."

Hubert, who was never backward when food was in

sight, had joined her, and already the dishes of cakes were beginning to diminish. Some of them bore little labels with the legends, "First prize," "Second prize," "Third prize," but they ignored these. Hubert, who had a passion for jam, crossed over to the jam table and emptied several pots of jam in the space of a few minutes. William, thinking that, as he would be blamed for the crime, he might as well share in its profits, found the dish of his mother's cakes (it bore a label Highly Commended) and ate them all. He found them very good but on the whole less enjoyable than in the raw state.

"Well, that was a *lovely* magic meal," said the little girl at last, "but I couldn't eat any more so let's go now."

Hubert, who had eaten one jar of jam too many, expressed himself also ready to go.

William threw an anxious glance round the room. Several of the dishes were quite empty. He moved a few cakes from other dishes on to them, put the empty jars of jam under the table, and hoped for the best.

They went out, and William drew a sigh of relief when he found the village street as empty as the Hall. No one had seen them go in. No one had seen them go out. The crime might after all not be discovered. They walked on.

Dorinda, insatiable as all her sex, demanded from William further proof of his magic power. She asked him to turn the lamppost into a prince in a cloak of gold and a diamond crown. William informed her rather curtly that his supply of magic was only sufficient for one spell a day. She accepted the explanation quite simply, obviously believing implicitly in his magic powers. Hubert was bewildered and annoyed.

Dorinda ignored him. It was evident that no one existed for Dorinda except William. She questioned him eagerly and unceasingly about his magic powers. Hubert, after enduring this for several minutes, made a bold bid for her attention.

"I can tell you a lot more about Munich," he said, "there's a big lake just near it where——"

"Do be quiet," said Dorinda. "I'm not a bit interested in the silly place."

"But you said you were," he protested.

"That was only because we'd got to write an essay on the place where we'd spent our holidays, and I thought I'd get more marks if I'd spent it abroad."

"But you didn't," said Hubert.

"No, silly, but if I wrote about the place you were talking about she'd think I had, wouldn't she? But it sounded a stupid place—*heaps* stupider than Swanage, so I'm going to stick to Swanage after all. . . ." She turned to William: "And can you do anything you like with your spell?"

"Well, some days it's stronger than others," said William anxious to guard against future contingencies. "Some days it's quite weak and I can only do *very* little things with it."

"It was *very* strong to-day, wasn't it?" said Dorinda with a sigh of blissful reminiscence. "I've never tasted such nice cakes before."

William remembered with an apprehensive qualm that Dorinda had eaten the entire contents of the dish that bore the label "Special Award of Honour." She had an appetite that her appearance of graceful fragility somehow did not suggest. William had filled up the dish with cakes from other exhibits, but he had an uneasy conviction that the matter would not end there.

"Anyone could *tell* they were magic cakes by the taste of them," went on Dorinda fervently.

Then Hubert brought out the bombshell he had been carefully preparing.

"I did laugh when I saw you running away from Farmer Jenks' bull the other day," he said casually to William.

William was taken aback. He certainly had fled precipitately when he realised that Farmer Jenks' bull was in the field with him, but he had not known that there was a witness of his flight. Hubert had seen him and was keeping the story till it could be used most effectively against him.

"Well," he said indignantly, "*everyone* runs away from a bull."

"I don't," said Hubert.

"Oh don't you!" said William. "Well I've seen you." Memory came to his aid. "I saw you in this *very* field, an' as soon as you saw that the bull was in it and coming to you, you ran into that shed and shut the door an' hid in it."

Hubert laughed.

"That was all you saw, wasn't it? You didn't see me come out of the shed and chase the bull across the field, did you?"

"No, I didn't."

"Well, that's what I did after you'd gone on."

"Well, why did you run into the shed, then?"

"Jus' to lure it on. To make it come right up to the shed door after me so that I could burst out at it an' chase it right across the field."

There was no doubt that Hubert had an imagination

that almost rivalled William's in fertility, and there was no doubt that Dorinda was unduly (as William considered in this case) credulous.

"Oh, Hubert, *did* you?" she said.

"Yes," said Hubert.

"I didn't see you," put in William.

"No 'cause you'd gone on. I waited till you'd gone on."

"An' you chased it *right* across the field, Hubert?" said Dorinda admiringly.

It was obvious that she had quite forgotten William's powers of magic in this new thrill of Hubert's powers of bullchasing. It was not William's first lesson in the fickleness of woman.

"Yes," said Hubert with his unbearable swagger.

"And was it really this field?" said Dorinda.

"Yes," said Hubert.

"And was that the shed?" said Dorinda pointing to a small shed in a corner of the field.

"Yes," said Hubert.

William looked round. A thick-set animal was making its way across the field in their direction.

"And that's the bull," he said.

Without a moment's hesitation the three of them took to their heels and fled across to the shed. There came behind them as they ran the thud of pounding hoofs. They slammed the door of the shed and bolted it. From beneath the door came the sound of heavy breathing. They could see a fraction of the nostril of their foe beneath it as he made vain efforts to get to his victims. Hubert's face had assumed a sea-green tint. William was panting. Only Dorinda was serene, untroubled. She turned to Hubert with the eager smile of one to whom the best is yet to come.

" You've lured him to the shed, Hubert," she said, " now go out and chase him across the field."

There was no sarcasm in her tone. She had firmly believed Hubert's story. It had never once occurred to her that their flight was not in the nature of a ruse in order to give Hubert the chance of chasing the bull across the field again.

"Go on, Hubert," she said, "go out and chase him."

She was dancing about in her eager anticipation of the joy of watching Hubert chase the bull.

"Chase him like you chased him the other day," she said. "Hurry up. He's still outside. I can hear him. Throw open the door and give him a fright and chase him right across the field. I'm *longing* for it."

Hubert turned his sea-green face to her.

"Don't be such a fool," he said.

Her eager excitement died away.

"Aren't you *going* to, Hubert?" she said.

"Course I'm not."

Disillusion clouded the blue eyes. She spoke in a small sad voice.

"Hubert, didn't you—didn't you chase it the other time?"

"Course I didn't," snapped Hubert.

Then suddenly his fat sea-green face broke up. "Boo hoo!" he sobbed, "I'm frightened. You oughtn't ever to have let me come into this field. It's all your fault. Boo hoo!"

Dorinda stared at him in amazement. Then she turned to William and something of her glow returned.

" *You'll* do it, William, won't you?" she said.

"What?" said William feebly.

"Chase him away. You know you said you'd

fought smugglers.   A bull isn't *half* as much trouble to
fight as smugglers.''

She gazed at him eagerly, imploringly, and yet with
something of apprehension, as if having once tasted
disillusionment she couldn't be quite sure of not tasting
it again.

William looked at the sea-green blubbing face of
Hubert and felt suddenly that any fate was preferable
to that of sharing in its shame, of bringing the crest-
fallen look of disillusionment again into Dorinda's
blue eyes.

"All right," he said airily, "I'll go 'n' chase him
all right."

Without stopping for a second to consider his
decision, he opened the door, stepped out and closed it
behind him.   He was alone in the field facing the bull.
To his surprise the bull did not attack him at once.   It
curvetted about for a few moments, then wheeled round
suddenly and went pounding back across the field.
William's rôle was open to him and he fulfilled it
instinctively.   He set off at a run, and Dorinda and
Hubert, who had opened the door, beheld the amazing
spectacle of William pursuing the bull across the field.
Half-way across, the bull stopped and faced him, again
curvetted heavily, then wheeled round and set off at a
run again.   William followed.   The gate leading from
the field to the farm yard was open.   The bull disappeared into the farm yard.   William pursued it to the
gate, where he was stopped by the sudden appearance
of Farmer Jenks' youngest daughter, a damsel of
pleasing appearance with none of her father's surliness
of disposition.   She smiled pleasantly at William.

"Father *will* be mad that you've found out," she
said.

"FATHER *WILL* BE MAD THAT YOU'VE FOUND OUT,"
SHE SAID.

"Found out what?" said William breathless from
his run.

"About Sammy."

"Who's Sammy?" said William.

"The bull," laughed the damsel. "You see, his

mother died when he was born, and we girls have brought him up, and he's as sweet tempered as a lamb, and loves a romp like a puppy. But father always wants you boys to think he's fierce, 'cause of keeping you out of his fields. How did you find out?"

William collected his scattered forces and assumed a knowing and superior air.

"Oh, I know a lot about bulls," he said. "I can always tell whether bulls are fierce or not," and added hastily, not wishing to lose the credit for superhuman valour in claiming that of superhuman knowledge: "Not that I'm afraid of any ole bull however savage it is. I jus' get hold of their horns and twist 'em on to the ground by 'em so's they can't move."

The girl laughed, and gave him an apple, and told him to get out of the field quick before father came home. Then she shut the gate and disappeared. William swaggered back across the field to where Dorinda, starry eyed and ecstatic, and Hubert, still sea-green and blubbing, were coming from the shed to meet him. He presented the apple to Dorinda with a courtly air.

"Oh William," she sighed blissfully, "it was *lovely* to watch you. I *knew* you would. What was the girl saying to you?"

"She was telling me what a jolly fierce bull it was, and that no one had ever chased it before," said William.

They walked home slowly, and William beguiled the time by describing from imagination other and more terrific encounters with bulls in which he somewhat monotonously played the part of hero. Hubert recovered from his epilepsy of fear, and began to explain that he would have chased the bull himself if he hadn't had cramp in his leg, and that he'd just been on the point of going out to chase it when William had forestalled him. Dorinda ignored him, demanding still more stories from the heroic William. Her credulity and his imagination were well matched.

They had retraced their steps to the Village Hall. William's instinct was to slink past it as inconspicuously as possible, but Dorinda expressed surprise to see it still standing there.

"I should have thought that it would have vanished as soon as we'd finished with it," she said. "Let's go in and see if there's any of the magic food left. I'm quite hungry again."

Reluctantly William followed her into the Hall. The scene was not the peaceful scene that usually met the eyes and ears of visitors to the Women's Guild Exhibitions. The sounds of fierce reproaches rent the air. A tall athletic-looking woman was angrily brandishing an empty jam jar (one of Hubert's efforts), which she had found under the table, and shouting at the top of her voice. Others brandished prize tickets and dishes, also shouting at the tops of their voices. The scene was chaotic.

Most of their anger seemed to be directed against a woman in a blue overall wearing a steward's badge, who was standing at bay against a trestle table, defending herself hysterically.

"No, I've no explanation. I don't know how it happened. Yes, I was left alone in charge for an hour just before it opened. Yes, I did leave it for a short time . . . well, I only just slipped down to the chemist. They shouldn't have made me judge the pickles . . . pickles never did suit me . . . I was in *agony*. I only went for some bicarbonate of soda. I didn't stay long . . . not very long. He had to go upstairs to his

store room for some . . . No, I didn't lock the door
when I was away . . . no one was about and I only
meant to be away a second and one can't think of
everything and I was in *agony*. No, I didn't notice
anything wrong when I got back. No, of course I
didn't examine everything. It was almost time to
open the door and I was still in agony. I still *am* in
agony. I think he'd had the stuff in stock too long, it
didn't seem to have any effect on me at all. I shall be
a wreck for life after this . . . some of the pickled onions
were practically *raw*. How *can* I tell you what
happened . . .? I don't *know* what happened. . . ."
She stopped for breath and an angry babel of voices
broke out again.

"Here's my cakes on a dish with a first prize label
with someone else's name on. My cakes got first prize
and they've made a mistake in the name."

"Pardon *me*, it's *my* name and the prize is for *my*
cakes."

"Well, where *are* your cakes?"

"The person who took them away should know
that."

"How *dare* you! . . . You never sent in any cakes.
You forged a prize ticket."

The raging individual with the empty jam jar pushed
them on one side and took the stage.

"*Slaved* over it I did! Best jam for miles around!
Everyone says so! *Sure* of the prize, I was. And
where do I find it? Emptied and stuck under a table.
I'll find who did it if I die, and I'll have their eyes out.
There's been some dirty work here and——"

A scream interrupted her. Hubert had thoughtfully
filled his every pocket with cakes and biscuits on his
previous visit to the Hall. Feeling hungry and shaken

and quite unaware of the meaning of the uproar around him, he now absently took out a cake and began to munch it.   A woman standing near him recognised her missing masterpiece and raised a scream.   They fell upon Hubert and emptied his pockets.   Hubert had a good eye for pastries and every one of the cakes they took from him had been a prize winner.   Each one was greeted with screams of anguished recognition by its creator.   Chaos and babel were redoubled.   Hubert in terror twisted himself from the hold of his captors, and fled out of the Hall followed by a crowd of enraged women.   The uproar died away in the distance. Peace descended upon the Hall with its small crowd of disinterested non-exhibitors who had merely come to see the exhibition.   And soon another sensation ran through the company like fire among stubble set going by a careless word of Dorinda's.   It was the sensation of William and the bull.   The story increased in picturesqueness and variation as it spread from mouth to mouth.   Dorinda herself had confused several of the details of what actually happened with details of the imaginary bull exploits that William had related to her on the way home.

According to one rumour William had seized hold of the horns of the bull just as it was going to toss him, and, being flung upon its back by the toss, had kept his seat there and guided the animal back to the farm yard.   According to another he had wrestled with it. According to another he had quelled it with the power of the human eye.   According to another he had been gored horribly and was now lying at the point of death in the Cottage Hospital.   The sight of his extremely healthy figure had a depressing effect on this rumour, but, as he could not be seen by everyone in the room at once, did not actually kill it. An eager and credulous crowd surrounded him, demanding details. He gave them freely. Then, just as he was describing how the bull had slunk through the gate of the field with its tail between its legs after he had wrestled with it and thrown it, he heard the sound of the returning crowd of exhibitors and decided that the moment had come for him to take his departure. Dorinda followed him.

"Why are you running so fast, William?" she said, trying to keep up with him.

"Jus' 'cause I like runnin'," said William breathlessly.

When he had reached a safe distance from the Village Hall he stopped.

"What were all those people making such a noise about?" said Dorinda.

"Oh, they jus' like makin' a noise," said William.

"I expect they were *frightfully* grateful to you for making all that magic food for them, weren't they?"

"I expect so," said William.

"I expect that was what they were all so excited about," said Dorinda; "I wonder where Hubert is?"

"He went for a little run too," said William.

"By himself?"

"Yes."

"I don't care. I'd rather be without him. I like you *heaps* better than Hubert."

"An' I like you heaps better than most girls I know," said William.

They had reached the end of the road where Hubert's house stood.

"I've got to go now," said Dorinda regretfully. "I'm only staying here to-day you know. Father's fetching me after tea an' it must be tea-time now."

"Well good-bye," said William brusquely.

"Good-bye, William. I think you're the bravest person in the world, and I think your magic's *wonderful* and I love you *ever* so much."

She raised her face and kissed him. She was unexpectedly pleasant to kiss. Then she waved her hand and disappeared down the lane.

William went on. He had decided to go for a long walk. Probably the leading part he had played in the Women's Guild Cookery Exhibition had been discovered by now, and it would be as well to keep out of the way in case instruments of justice were already searching for him. He hoped that the story of his exploit with the bull would have the effect of tempering justice with mercy, but he didn't really care. He thought of Dorinda's gaze of admiration, of her unexpectedly pleasant kiss, of the delicious feast of prize home-made cakes, of Hubert, sea-green and blubbing, of the fascinating feeling of pursuing a bull across a field . . . and he felt that nothing on earth could take the savour from these memories.

He took a stick from the hedge and swaggered along the road, singing loudly to himself and slashing the stick through the air.

In front of him fled thousands of imaginary bulls, their tails between their legs.

CHAPTER VII

THE OUTLAWS AND THE MISSIONARY

IT was Mrs. Monks, the Vicar's wife, who insisted on holding a drawing-room missionary meeting for children the day after she had held the drawing-room missionary meeting for grown-ups. She was a woman whose zeal sometimes outran her discretion, and she was also a frugal woman who did not like to see good cakes and sandwiches wasted. She approached the Outlaws' parents first of all, and the Outlaws' parents, though not enthusiastic, could not bring any valid reason against her proposal. Their lack of enthusiasm was due to a conviction, born of experience, that things in which their sons took part generally ended disastrously, rather than to any definite flaw in the project itself.

"But how *can* it do any harm?" said Mrs. Monks. "They'll come to tea, and he'll just talk to them and ask them *all* to try to collect some money, and then he'll have another meeting in a fortnight's time and they can give in their money."

So the Outlaws' parents reluctantly acquiesced, and four brushed and scoured boys went to swell the ranks of Mrs. Monks's juvenile missionary meeting.

"Waste of an afternoon," grumbled William moodily.

"There'll be tea anyway," said Ginger, trying to look on the bright side.

"Yes, what they left yesterday," said William, "an'

it'll all be stale, an' not enough, an' she'll not give us any more. I know her. The last eatin' up tea I came to of hers I only got one piece of bread and butter, an' it was as hard as nails, an' all curled up."

"*An'* listenin' to a dull ole lecture all the time," said Ginger. "I'm *sick* of lectures. It's only a week ago we had one on stars at school an' I was too far back to hear a word he said, an' those that could said I was jolly lucky."

But the gloomy forebodings of the Outlaws were not justified. The tea was ample and the lecturer not only audible but inspiring. He stirred the competitive instinct that is such a potent factor with the young. He ended his speech by saying: "You must each try to collect two shillings, but you mustn't stop at the two shillings, you know. Now let us see which of all you boys and girls can bring me the most money to our next meeting."

And at once the Outlaws felt that their honour demanded that they should beat all the other competitors and bring the largest amount of money to the next meeting. It didn't matter whether it was a question of good deeds or ill, of success in trespassing or fighting or missionary work, the Outlaws liked to lord it over their contemporaries.

They went straight to the old barn to discuss the matter. William was the only one of them who had any money, and he had fourpence, but he lost no time in informing them that his fourpence was not eligible as the nucleus of their new fund.

"I'd saved it for a new pistol," he explained, "one like Victor Jameson's got. They're only fourpence but they'd sold the last one to Victor, but the man said he was havin' some more in an'" (putting the fourpence very firmly back into his pocket) "an' this four-pence is for the pistol when it comes, not for any ole savages. I'd 've spent it las' Saturday if he'd had a pistol in the shop, so I count it as spent 'cause it's only waitin' till the pistols come in."

The Outlaws admitted the justice of this.

"Yes, it wouldn't be fair to take your fourpence," said Ginger. "We'll get enough without that. We'll find some way of makin' money we've never tried before."

Their previous attempts at money-making had indeed been numerous but not strikingly successful.

"We've tried everything," said William. "We've tried shows and sellin' things to people an' doin' things for people, an' actin' plays an' writin' newspapers an' —an' everythin'. I don't think there is any way of makin' money that we've not tried."

"My aunt was readin' a story to me las' Sunday," said Henry. "I wasn't listenin' but I couldn't help hearin' bits now an' then an' it was about a girl that wanted some money for her sister that was starvin' an' she sold her hair."

"Her *what*?" said William incredulously.

"Her hair."

"Who to?"

"A hairdresser."

"*Well!*" said William amazed, "I never heard of anyone doin' that before. How much did he give for it."

"Five pounds," said Henry.

"Five—*what*!" said William.

"Five pounds."

"Crumbs!"

"It *must* be true if it's in a book," said Henry.

"Well, it's a jolly easy way of gettin' money if it's true," said William. "Let's go 'n try it. I say! Three fives are fifteen. What if he gives us fifteen pounds!"

Credulous as the Outlaws were, this hardly seemed

"WE'VE COME TO SELL YOU OUR HAIR," SAID WILLIAM. "WE'LL SELL IT FOR FIVE POUNDS THE LOT."

possible, but they were not prepared for the ridicule with which Mr. Theobald, the village barber, received their offer.

"We've come to sell you our hair," said William.

"*What?*" said Mr. Theobald.

"We'll sell you our hair. Five pounds the lot," said William generously, "the ordin'ry price is five pounds each, but we don't want to be mean, so we'll sell it at five pounds the lot."

Mr. Theobald threw back his bald head and roared with laughter. He went into his little saloon and told it to his customers. He went to his front door and proclaimed it to the village street.

"I'll cut it for sixpence each," he said to the Outlaws at the end, "and not before it needs it either."

Loud laughter followed the Outlaws out of the shop. Loud laughter followed them down the village street. The joke was repeated from door to door. They heard Mr. Theobald repeating it in a raucous voice for the benefit of the further end of the village street. The doubled shouts of laughter accompanied them. The Outlaws marched on, their faces flaming angrily. They did not take kindly to being butts for ridicule.

In the old barn they sat down and considered this new complication that had invaded the situation.

"You know what he is when he gets hold of anything he thinks is funny," said William; "he'll tell it to everyone who goes into his shop an' everyone'll be laughing at us. All your aunt's fault," he ended moodily to Henry, "reading you stories that weren't true."

"Well, what're we goin' to *do*?" said Ginger.

The problem of wiping out this insult now filled the whole mental horizon of the Outlaws. They had quite forgotten the project for which they had wanted the money.

"We've gotter do somethin' to make people laugh at *him*," muttered Henry.

William thought of Mr. Theobald—saw him in his mind's eye standing as he stood every morning in his shop doorway, the sun shining on his bald head, beneath his sign: "THEOBALD HAIRDRESSER."

And William's face was lit suddenly as by a light from within.

"I know what we'll do," he said, "we only want a bit of black paint and a ladder, and there's both in our toolshed."

The next morning the men who hurried down the village street towards the station went shaking and guffawing on their way. For Mr. Theobald stood in his doorway as usual, the sun shining on his bald head. But William and the Outlaws had come after dark with a ladder and a pot of black paint, and the sign above his head now ran: "THE BALD HAIRDRESSER." Mr. Theobald was not annoyed by the laughter. He was still engaged in broadcasting the story of the Outlaws' offer and he took the laughter as tribute to the jest.

It was not till almost lunch time that he realised that the laughter that still resounded through the village street was connected in any way with himself.

That little affair settled, the Outlaws turned their attention again to the matter of the money for the missionaries. If Mr. Theobald would not buy their hair, they must find some other way of making money. They discussed every method they could think of, and dismissed each as impossible. They had almost given up hope when Douglas found a page of his mother's cookery book on the floor of the dining-room, and, picking it up, began to read it simply because at the time he happened to have nothing else to do.

At once he summoned another meeting of the Outlaws in the old barn.

"Look," he said eagerly, "it tells you how to make ginger beer an' it sounds quite easy. An' *everyone* likes ginger beer. I bet if we make ginger beer an' sell it, we'll get a lot of money."

"How do you make it?" said William.

"You only want ginger an' water an' sugar an' lemon an' yeast," he said, and ended simply, "an' they're all things we can get from our homes without anyone knowin' they've gone."

The Outlaws took up the idea with enthusiasm. It was decided that Ginger should get the yeast from his home, Henry the sugar, Douglas the ginger, and William the lemon.

"An' we'll start collectin' bottles at once," said William. "I bet we ought to make enough to conquer all the savages in the world."

Despite the eloquence of the missionary, the Outlaws were still somewhat vague as to his exact aims.

A motley crew of bottles was assembled in the old barn, and the Outlaws viewed them with pride.

"I bet we'll get more money this way than anyone," said William optimistically. "I bet we'll keep on doin' it afterwards too an' have a bit of money for ourselves for a change. An' then when we're grown up we can have a ginger beer shop an' I bet we end up as millionaires."

Ginger, who had purloined a basin from home, was already engaged upon the manufacture.

"I'm puttin' a *lot* of yeast in," he said, "because that's what makes it fizzy."

It was a proud moment for the Outlaws when they stood by the roadside, their strange assortment of bottles displayed on a board, with a notice "Ginger beer tuppence a bottel. Made by us," elegantly designed in paints of many colours by Henry. It was by no means the first time that the Outlaws had had a stall by the roadside, but it was the first time that they had actually manufactured the wares they were selling. There was no lack of customers, and the bottles of ginger beer had all gone in less than an hour. In fact, the Outlaws were already manufacturing another supply in the old barn, when the crowd of enraged customers ran them to earth, demanding their money back. It appeared that all the bottles had exploded either on the way home or as soon as they reached home. One customer had been hit in the eye by the cork. Another had had her coat ruined. The father of another had been caught by a piece of flying glass. The cat of another had been so terrified by the report that it had shot out of the house like an arrow from a bow and so far all search for it had proved fruitless. The baby brother of another had been drenched in ginger beer. The fact that he had been intensely amused by the episode and had called out "'gain!" detracted nothing from his mother's indignation. One cork had smashed an electric-light bulb and another a valuable vase. Had the customers come back alone the Outlaws might possibly have been a match for them, but they didn't. They brought indignant parents in their train—the parents whose vases and bulbs had been broken and whose babies had been drenched in ginger beer. The parents did not merely demand the money back. They extracted it violently from the Outlaws' pockets, telling them many forcible home truths in the process.

When they had gone, the Outlaws sat and looked

at each other blankly.   "Well," said William bitterly,
"talk about *savages*!"

Then he turned out his pocket and found the four
pennies still intact.

"I DON'T REALLY WANT THE MIXTURE, SO YOU'D BETTER
PUT IT IN THE GREENHOUSE," SAID DOUGLAS'S AUNT.

"Wonder they didn't take *that* while they were about it," he said ironically, "well, nothin' on *earth'd* make me give missionaries these four pennies now."

Henry turned his sorrowful gaze to the mixture that stood in a corner of the old barn.

"What're we goin' to do with that?" he said.

"Tell you what," said Douglas, "let's try my aunt.

WITH GLEE THE OUTLAWS WATCHED THE MONEY PASS
TO WILLIAM'S READY HAND.

I bet she doesn't like ginger beer, but she's jolly keen on missionaries an' savages an' things like that. She's gone away to-day, but she'll be back to-morrow afternoon. We'll take 'em round to-morrow afternoon."

To-morrow afternoon was the afternoon of the meeting, and the Outlaws felt that it was running it rather close, but their usual optimism upheld them, and they set off hopefully, early the next afternoon, to Douglas's aunt's house with a wheelbarrow full of bottles.

Douglas's aunt disliked boys and was on far from friendly terms with Douglas, but she was, as Douglas had said, "keen on missionaries an' savages an' things like that," and she was deeply touched by their errand.

"I think it's splendid of you, boys," she said, "and I do hope that it means that your conduct's going to be *completely* different in the future. I do hope that, now you've turned your thoughts and interest to *serious* things, we shan't have so much to complain of in you. This is a *very* good sign, and I'm only too glad to give my subscription to the Cause through you."

She opened her purse and gave William three half-crowns.

"I don't really want the mixture, of course, so you'd better put it in the greenhouse to be out of the way."

They put it in the greenhouse, and went quickly away. A muffled report from the greenhouse, followed by the sound of breaking glass, reached them as they shut the gate.

"Seven an' six," said William blissfully, when they had reached a safe distance from Douglas's aunt's house, "I bet no one'll have more than that."

Victor Jameson passed on the other side of the street.

"Hi!" called William, "how much have you got for the savages?"

"Seven an' six," called Victor proudly, "an' I bet you've not got more'n' that."

"Oh, *haven't* we?" returned William, but the faces of the Outlaws had fallen.

They waited till Victor was out of earshot, then Ginger said:

"Well, we won't have the most after all."

"Yes, we jolly well will," said William firmly, "*an'* we won't use my fourpence either."

"How'll we do it?" demanded Ginger.

"We'll have to think out some way," said William the unconquerable.

At that moment another group of boys passed. They too had been at the missionary meeting.

"How much have you got?" shouted William.

"Five shillings," shouted the boys proudly. "I bet *you've* not got 's much as that."

"Oh, haven't we," said William, "well, where're you goin' now? It's not time for the meeting yet, is it?"

"No, there's a fair in Jenks's meadow, didn't you know?"

"No."

"Well, it's only a little one. There isn't even a proper merry-go-round. Only swings an' coconut shies an' things like that. There's jus' time to go round it before the meetin' begins."

"Come on," said William to his Outlaws, promptly forgetting everything but the fair; "we needn't spend any money there."

It was, as the boys had said, only a little fair, but the Outlaws wandered round it with great enjoyment.

One item of it interested them especially. It was called the Stock Exchange machine. You put a penny in the slot and the pointer whirled round the dial. If it stopped at the name of certain commodities your penny was returned with another. If it stopped at the name of others nothing happened. As the Outlaws stood round it a man put in a penny. The finger moved round to "Coal" and twopence came back through the slot. The man pocketed it and went away. William's eyes gleamed.

"I say," he said, "that's the way to do it. We'll get double what Douglas's aunt gave us. What'll it be?"—he wrestled mentally with the terrific sum and finally emerged victorious—"it'll be fifteen shillings. I say, won't Victor be sold when we say we've got fifteen shillings!" He took one of the half-crowns out of his pocket. "Well, the first thing is to change this into pennies."

*   *   *   *   *

The children streamed into the Vicarage and ranged themselves on benches under the direction of the Vicar's wife. The Vicar's wife was a good woman, but she disliked children, and it was only a strong sense of duty that made her have the children's affairs at all. It was the Outlaws, of course, that she dreaded most, and, as she superintended the ranging of the children on the benches, her eyes were anxiously fixed on the doorway by which they should enter. At last they came and as soon as she saw them her heart lightened. It was quite evident that they were not in an obstreperous mood. They entered moodily, gloomily, their brows set, their eyes fixed on the floor. They took their places in the marshalled rows of their contemporaries without even scuffling. They had with them no

"YOU OWE US FOURPENCE," SAID WILLIAM STERNLY
TO THE MISSIONARY.

musical instruments with which to beguile the monotony of the meeting. They forbore even to move away the chairs of their neighbours as they sat down. They sat silent, gloomy, and scowling, waiting for the missionary to enter. He entered, smiling and debonair.

"Now, children," he said, "I'll ask you in turn how much each of you have got for the Cause, and then you will come up one by one and present it to me, and I will give you a receipt for the amount with a beautiful picture that you can have framed. . . ."

"Now," he began with Victor Jameson, "how much have you got?"

Victor Jameson proudly said "seven and sixpence," and, after a few words of commendation, the missionary passed on to the next. It was at this point that William began to burrow in his pocket and to realise for the first time that he had not only lost all Douglas's aunt's money at the Stock Exchange machine, but also his own precious fourpence. The missionary had reached him now.

"And you, my little man," he said, "you were collecting in a group of four, weren't you? How much have you got?"

William's hands had just finished their search for the missing fourpence, and his gloom had changed to indignation.

He fixed a stern eye upon the missionary.

"Nothing, and you owe us fourpence," he said.

The smile dropped from the missionary's face.

"W-what?" he gasped.

"You owe us fourpence," said William. "We've tried to get a lot of money for you, but we've lost fourpence of our own on it, so you owe us fourpence."

"I don't know what you mean," said the missionary. "How much money have you actually got?"

"I've told you," said William, "nothing, and you owe us fourpence."

The Vicar's wife rose from her seat, and the Outlaws were ignominiously ejected, William still loudly protesting that the missionary owed them fourpence.

Outside the Vicarage gate William gazed at his Outlaws indignantly.

"That's the last thing I ever do for missionaries," said William, "if they don't pay their debts they can't *expect* people to help them."

The Outlaws agreed and the four of them walked gloomily down the village street. They had avoided the village street since their encounter with Mr. Theobald, but they had forgotten that in this last blow of Fate.

"I can't even get that pistol now." grumbled William, "and I don't know if I'll ever have another fourpence. I don't wonder the savages eat them."

By "them" he was referring not to pistols or fourpences but to missionaries. "It's the same as stealin' not payin' debts," he went on fiercely.

Then they glanced across the street.

Mr. Theobald stood in his doorway. Just over his head the O of Theobald—staringly new and golden— flashed in the sun.

Mr. Theobald looked at the Outlaws. He had been feeling slightly depressed and rheumaticky, but the sight of the Outlaws cheered him. He had completely forgotten the trick that had been played on his sign, but he remembered the Outlaws' offer to sell him their hair for five pounds, and he burst into peals of laughter remembering it.

The Outlaws looked at him.

They had completely forgotten their offer to sell him their hair, but they remembered the glorious trick they had played on him. Their laughter answered his across the village street.

Mr. Theobald turned back into his shop. His depression and his rheumatism had left him suddenly. "A jolly good joke," he said to himself, "I shall see those boys standing there and saying: 'We'll sell you our hair for five pounds the lot,' till my dying day."

"Never mind," said William to the Outlaws as they passed on, "what's fourpence? And the pistol'd only get broke. And I'm jolly glad we'd not got any money for that man. I say, whenever I think of him standing there with THE BALD HAIRDRESSER over him, I simply can't stop laughing."

Laughing heartily, the Outlaws passed on their way.

CHAPTER VIII

THE OUTLAWS AND THE TRAMP

THE Outlaws wandered slowly down the road. It was Saturday afternoon and they were on their way to the woods with Jumble at their heels. They were discussing that subject of perennial interest—the uselessness of school.

"You never see my father sitting down to do French or any of the things he learnt to do at school," said William eloquently, "so I don't see what good it did him. Nor any of us."

"You've gotter learn to read and write, of course," said Ginger, with the air of one who wishes to be absolutely impartial. "I quite see *that*. You've gotter learn to read so as to be able to read story books, an' you've gotter learn to write so as to be able to write letters to people to thank 'em for sending you presents, 'cause if you don't they don't send any more, an' you've gotter know a bit of arithmetic so as to be able to tell if they give you wrong change in shops, but that's all. I think that when you can read and write and know enough arithmetic to know when you're getting wrong change in shops you ought to be able to leave school. That's what I think. I think all this Latin an' French an' geography's wrong. I——"

They had turned a bend in the road and there on the roadside before them sat a tramp. He was a gloriously unkempt tramp with long, red hair and a straggling, red beard. He wore the brim of an old straw hat at a jaunty angle. His coat may have first seen life at a fashionable wedding in the 'eighties. His trousers had obviously attended race meetings in their prime. His boots were tied on with string. It was clear that both the clothes and their wearer had seen better days though not in each other's company. He was cooking something over a smoky fire and singing in a deep bass voice. The Outlaws stood around him.

"Hello, my boys," he greeted them cheerfully. "Where are you off to with that fine dog?"

William's heart warmed to him. So few people perceived the fineness of Jumble at first sight like this. The first sight of Jumble—a dog of multiple pedigree—more often excited scorn and derision. William was quite accustomed to doing battle on Jumble's behalf against scoffers, as the knights of old did battle for their ladies. The "fine dog" proved the tramp a man of perspicacity and understanding.

"Can we stay and watch you?" said William.

"Come on," said the tramp genially. "Sit down and welcome, young gents. . . ."

They sat round in a semi-circle and watched the progress of the tramp's meal. He drank the steaming concoction straight from the tin. Then from a large flapping pocket he drew half a loaf and a pocket-knife and a newspaper "screw" containing cheese. Having eaten this with gusto, he drew from another part of his person a bottle whose contents he drank with even greater gusto. Then he took out a short, black clay pipe, filled it, lit it, and lay back on the path with a sigh of content, his head on his hands, gazing up at the sky.

William broke the spell-bound silence with which they had watched him.

"Can anybody be one?" he said eagerly.

"Be one what?" said the tramp.

"A tramp," said William. "We'd all like to be them."

The tramp's eyes twinkled under their bushy, red eyebrows. "It's not an easy life," he said, but he looked so carefree and merry as he said it that the Outlaws didn't believe him for a second.

"You can do jus' what you like, can't you?" said Ginger. "Climb trees and paddle and have fights and things like that?"

"Oh, yes," said the tramp.

"And go where you like," said Douglas enthusiastically.

"And eat when you like," said Henry.

"When you've got it," agreed the tramp.

"And wear what you like," said William, gazing with admiration at the fluttering rags and the boots tied on with string.

"Oh, yes," said the tramp.

"And people aren't always making you wash and brush your hair," said Ginger, "and telling you not to get your feet wet."

"No," agreed the tramp, stroking his straggling locks. "I can't say they are."

"Well," said William earnestly, holding back Jumble, who was showing signs of dislike of their new friend, despite his opening compliment, "how do you get *in* to it? How can you *be* one?"

The tramp shook his head.

"It's not easy," he said.

"I suppose we can't till we're grown up," said

William, "but what we want to know is how to get into it *then*. 'Cause I bet we all want to start the minute we're twenty-one, don't we?" he said to the others.

The others agreed—all but Jumble who uttered a dissentient growl.

"Well," said the tramp confidentially, "it's more difficult than people think. It's not generally known in fact that it's as difficult to get into as many of the other professions."

"If you've gotter pass examinations in not washin' an' in eatin' like you do," said William, "I bet we'd soon pass 'em."

The tramp shook his head.

"No, it's not that," he said, "this is one of the professions you've got to pay your way into."

The faces of the Outlaws fell. Their hands went instinctively into their empty pockets.

"Now I'll tell you all about it," said the tramp kindly, motioning them into a closer circle. They drew around, wide-eyed with eager interest. "Now it's like this," went on the tramp. "There are just a few of us at the head and we manage everything. We only admit a certain number of people to the profession each year, because, of course, it wouldn't be the grand life it is if there was too many of us." His voice sank to a sinister whisper. "People who try to set up as tramps on their own just—disappear." He uttered this word in a blood-curdling hiss and at the same time drew his finger along his throat from ear to ear. The eyes of the Outlaws started still further from their heads, and they moved yet nearer, thrilled to the core of their lawless beings.

"We've gotter be *merciless* in a profession like ours,"

went on the tramp, "otherwise it would go to pieces at once. Now if you young gents really want to get into it——"

The Outlaws assured him in an eager chorus that they did. "Well then, all I can say is that you're lucky to have met me. I'm the head of the whole tramp profession an' no one can get into it 'cept through me."

The Outlaws heaved deep sighs of ecstasy. Their future life seemed to stretch before them, bathed in a roseate glow. They saw themselves gloriously unwashed and unbrushed, roaming the countryside, cooking strange picnic meals on fires they had made themselves, going to bed as late as they liked, climbing trees, sleeping in barns or by the roadside.

"Now I'm goin' to do what I can for you," went on the tramp. "If I pass you into the profession, as it were, then we'll give you all our tips. We'll tell you the best places for sleeping and getting your meals. We'll tell you the places where the people'll give you food and the places where they won't, and we'll tell you the woods where you can poach safely and the woods where you can't."

Again a visible thrill of excitement passed through the Outlaws. Even Jumble showed signs of interest.

"But," went on the tramp, "there's got to be a sort of entrance fee, of course. You pay us a fee and we pass you in and hand on all our secrets to you. It's only fair, isn't it?"

The Outlaws agreed that it was, but their spirits had fallen and again their hands went to their empty pockets, hoping against hope to find some overlooked coin in them.

"How much is it?" said William anxiously.

The tramp swept a speculative glance over them, then said: "Two shillings each."

There was a sudden dejected silence. Then Ginger said hopefully:

"Well, we can't start till we're grown up and we're sure to have two shillings each when we're grown up."

The tramp shook his head sadly as if loth to curb their optimism.

"I'm afraid it's no use waiting till then," said the tramp. "You see, we've got what you might call a long waiting list. I mean, if you wait till you're grown up it will be too late. We can't have too many tramps. It would spoil the profession altogether. The only safe way of getting into it is to pay your entrance money when you're"—again his glance swept over them speculatively—"just the age you are now. Then when you're grown up and want to come on the road you'll find everything ready for you."

The Outlaws consulted together. "But we haven't got any money just now——" began William.

"*Tell* you what," interrupted the tramp good-humouredly. "I've taken a liking to you four. You're the sort we *want* on the road, see? I feel you'd be a credit to us." The Outlaws swelled visibly with pride. "I'll come back here in a week's time. Now that's a thing I've never done before. Always before I've given the candidate his chance once and for all. If he can pay his entrance fee he's in, and if he can't he'll never have a second chance. That's one of my rules. I never give anyone a second chance. But I'm going to break my rule with you. I'm going to come back here in a week's time. You'll be able to get the money by then, won't you?"

The Outlaws promised eagerly.

"Well, I'll be back in a week's time, and we'll meet here and you give me your entrance fees, and I'll give you an envelope containing an address that you must go to when you're ready to start in the profession. Now that's a thing I've never done for anyone else."

The Outlaws thanked him profusely. He held up his hand and continued impressively.

"There's only one condition," he said, "and that is that you keep this a secret between us. If any of you young gents breathe a word of this to anyone, then it's all over. You see, I don't want people to know that I've given anyone a second chance. It would be held up against me for the rest of my life. It would brand me as a weak man, which I'm not. It might even prevent me from coming to you next week with the address. So will each of you young gents give me your solemn promise not to breathe a word of this to anyone till we meet next week?"

The Outlaws promised solemnly. The tramp stowed away the remnants of his meal in his pockets, then rose, stretching himself luxuriously.

"Well," he said "this time next week we'll all meet here—you with your entrance money and me with the address. Mind you," he added, "I'm letting you off cheap. I charge most people half a crown. . . . But I like you young gents. Well—good-bye till next week."

He strolled off down the road, whistling gaily.

Jumble barked defiance at him from a safe distance. The Outlaws gazed after him with rapt admiration, till he had disappeared. Then once more they drew deep breaths of ecstasy.

"Fancy *that* happenin' to *us*!" said William at last.

"I'd like to be *jus'* like him," said Ginger earnestly.

"I'm goin' to tie my boots on with string same as him," said Douglas.

"It's more *possible* than pirates or Red Indians," said Henry. "I'm glad we've chosen it."

"Two shillings each," said William meditatively, "eight shillings altogether," and, appalled by the total, added "*Gosh!*"

"We've *got* to get it," said Ginger sternly.

"Of course we have," agreed William.

"It would be awful," said Douglas, "to have to be a doctor or lawyer or something like that when we grew up just for want of two shillings now."

"How shall we get it?" said Henry. "None of my family will give me any. They say they're not going to give me any till all the things my bomb broke are paid for. Well, I didn't mean it to go off till I'd finished making it. I was jus' making it quite quietly an' suddenly it went off. Well, anyway it must have been a jolly good bomb. It wouldn't have gone off if it hadn't been. I told them that they ought to be glad because it showed how useful I'd be in time of war but they said yes, to the enemy, and things like that, and said I'd got to pay for everything it broke, and it seemed to have chosen all the most expensive things in the room to break."

But the Outlaws were tired of Henry's bomb. Though the explosion had only taken place a few days ago he had dwelt on the subject so long and so eloquently that their sympathy and interest were exhausted. After all there was nothing unique in his experience. They had all made bombs with more or less similar results.

"Let's all go and see if we can get any money at home first," said William, "an' if we can't we'll have

to think of some other way of getting it.   We've *got* to
have it by this time next week," and added, again
appalled by the magnitude of the task before them:
"*Eight* shillings!   *Gosh!*"

"MOTHER, MAY I HAVE SOME MONEY, PLEASE?"
SAID WILLIAM HOPEFULLY.

William entered the drawing-room where his mother
sat engaged in her usual task of household mending.
She was just beginning on a sock of William's from
which the entire heel seemed to be missing.

"I wish you weren't so hard on them, dear," she said as he entered. "Couldn't you try to walk more lightly?"

"Uh-huh," said William vaguely, in an obliging tone of voice, then, sitting down by her, he said hopefully: "Mother, may I have some money, please?"

"What for, dear?" said Mrs. Brown, gazing with an abstracted frown at the cavity through which both her fist and the darning "mushroom" slipped so unavailingly. "I can't think what you do to them. These were new last month."

"I only walk in them same as other people," said William, coldly, and added: "Just to spend."

"But you've got your pocket-money, dear," said Mrs. Brown.

"No I haven't," said William simply, "I've spent it.   Besides, that's only twopence."

"How much do you want?" said Mrs. Brown, spanning the girth of the hole with a huge strand of wool.   "I wish one could patch them."

"Two shillings," said William.

"Two *shillings*!" said Mrs Brown. indignantly. "I never *heard* of such a thing, William.   Whatever do you want two shillings for?"

"It's something to do with my future," said William mysteriously.

"Nonsense!" said Mrs. Brown.   "You know I don't believe in fortune telling, and two shillings is an outrageous sum to charge for it any way.   You mustn't have it done."

"Have what done?"

"Your horoscope, dear, or whatever it is."

"I don't know what you mean," said William impatiently.   "All I want is two shillings for a reason that you ought to be very thankful for if you knew. Because it's going to save you a lot of money."

"How is it going to save me a lot of money, dear? And I do wish you'd stand out of the light. I'm sure Robert never made holes this size. Why need you walk so *heavily*?"

"I bet I've got a bit heavier brain than Robert ever had," said William. "Naturally a brain like mine soon goes through a bit of wool."

"But your brain isn't in your *heel*, William."

"No, but I've got to carry the weight of it on my heel when I walk, haven't I? If you don't want to have so much darning to do," he went on hopefully, "you ought to stop me going to school. Or at any rate let me stop learning Latin. I bet it's Latin that makes my brain so heavy."

"Nonsense, William, of course you can't stop learning anything."

"Well," sighed William, "don't blame me, then, if the weight of my brain goes through a bit of wool."

He remembered the errand he had come on and began another oblique attack.

"How much money would you have to spend on me being a doctor if I wanted to be one?"

"Do you want to be a doctor, dear?" said Mrs. Brown absently. "You'll have to work much harder at school and be a lot cleaner and tidier than you are before you can be a doctor."

"I don't want to be a doctor," said William, controlling his impatience with difficulty, "but how much do you have to spend to be a doctor?"

"Several hundred pounds, I believe," said Mrs. Brown vaguely.

"Well," said William with an air of one who is about to confer a great favour. "I'm goin' to save you all that money. If you give me two shillings now you needn't spend all that money making me a doctor."

"But no one was going to make you a doctor, dear," said Mrs. Brown. "It's never even been suggested. You've never mentioned it before. I'd no idea you wanted to be a doctor."

"I *don't* want to be a doctor," said William. "Only I've got to be *something*, haven't I? I mean, whatever I am you'll have to pay money to make me it, won't you?"

"I suppose so," sighed Mrs. Brown.

"Well, what I'm tryin' to tell you," said William, "is that I'm going to let you off all that money if you'll pay me two shillings now."

"William, what *nonsense!* You'll have to have some sort of career, I suppose, and it's sure to cost a lot of money, and you might think of that when you're so careless with your clothes, but paying two shillings now can't possibly make any difference to the money we'll have to pay for your career."

"Well, it can and it does," persisted William. "I've *got* a career already, an' two shillings'll get me into it, an' I can start straight on to it when I'm twenty-one, an' you'll never have any more trouble about me. I can't tell you all about it yet, 'cause I've promised not to, but—well," addressing the ceiling with bitter irony, "it seems a funny thing to me for a mother not even to want to pay two shillings to get her son into a career."

"Do run away, dear, and stop talking nonsense," said Mrs. Brown, exploring a second sock with a hand that again emerged into daylight through the place where William's heel had rested, "and you *will* keep standing in my light."

William went into the hall where he uttered a sarcastic laugh, then apostrophised the hat stand.

"That's the sort of mother *I've* got," he informed it. "Won't even give two shillings to get her son into a career."

The only other member of the family who was in the house was his sister, Ethel. He walked slowly up to her bedroom and knocked at the door. She said "Come in," and greeted him on his entry without enthusiasm. "Well, what do you want?"

He closed the door and went over to her window seat.

She was standing in front of her mirror, trying on a black hat. A green hat lay on her dressing-table. She took off the black hat and tried on the green one. Then she took off the green one and tried on the black one, studying her reflection the while with an anxious frown. It was obvious that she was endeavouring to decide which suited her the better.

"Ethel," said William portentously, "would you like to do something about my future?"

Ethel glanced at him still without enthusiasm.

"Yes, I would," she said grimly. "I'd like to do quite a lot about your future."

He remembered a slight misunderstanding that he had had with her the day before about a scarf that he had "borrowed" without her knowledge to use as a head band in his capacity as pirate chief. He had pointed out to her that it was not he but an enemy who had snatched it off his head and thrown it into a pond during a fight. He had pointed out that, if that had not happened, she would never even have known he had "borrowed" it, such care was he taking of it. She was still feeling annoyed about it, he supposed. Just like a girl. . . . Cunningly he approached a side of the question that might appeal to her in her present mood.

"How would you like never to see me again after I'm twenty-one, Ethel?" he said.

"It seems a long time to wait," said his sister.

He ignored the insult. "Well, if you'll give me two shillings," he said, "you'll never see me again after I'm twenty-one."

His sister was studying the effect of the green hat frowningly in the glass and didn't answer.

He repeated his offer.

"I think you're rather optimistic," she said. "Personally, I think you'll get put in prison long before you're twenty-one. By the way you go about treating other people's property as if it was yours I don't think you've got long to wait now."

"Crumbs!" he said. "I've never come across anything like the way you remember little things that no one else would ever think of again. It hasn't done it any harm. Water's *good* for things. . . . Anyway, I wasn't talking about prison. I was talking about a career. A jolly good career that you can get me into for two shillings. Well," he ended pathetically, "that's not much for a boy's only sister to do for him, is it? Just two shillings for his career."

"It's a jolly sight more than you'll ever get out of me," she said shortly.

William sighed at this further proof of feminine heartlessness and considered his next move.

Ethel tried on the black hat again, then returned so the green one. William's eyes roved round the room. Upon the chest of drawers near the window stood the

photograph of a good-looking young man in a silver
frame with the name "Jimmie" scrawled across it.
It was the only photograph in the room except for the

"IF YOU'LL GIVE ME TWO SHILLINGS," SAID WILLIAM, "YOU'LL
NEVER SEE ME AGAIN AFTER I'M TWENTY-ONE."

photograph of Mr. and Mrs. Brown on the mantelpiece.
A few weeks ago Ethel's room had been full of framed
photographs of eligible youths affectionately inscribed.
Ethel had been a girl of many affairs. It would be
difficult indeed for a girl to have hair of the exact red-

gold colour of Ethel's and eyes of the exact blue of
Ethel's, and a mouth with the appealing curve of
Ethel's, and not be a girl of many affairs.   Young men
fell in love with Ethel at first sight.   They smiled on
her and waited on her and swallowed her snubs with a
meekness that would have amazed their families.   And
Ethel was kind to them or cruel to them as the whim
seized her.   Then quite suddenly a young man named
Jimmie Moore appeared on her horizon and wrought a
complete change in her.   There wasn't any doubt at all
that Ethel for the first time in her life was in love.
And there was still less doubt that Jimmie was in
love. . . .

Ethel caught sight of Jimmie now entering the garden
gate, blushed, smiled, waved her hand, pulled on the
green hat (she looked equally pretty in either), and
started for the door.   As she passed the photograph
she stopped, gazed at it languishingly, then with a
sudden angry movement opened the top drawer, took
out an armful of the deposed photographs, flung them
scornfully into the fireplace, and departed.

William uttered his bitter laugh.   "Huh," he said.
"I bet she wouldn't mind givin' *him* two shillings to
start him on a career."

He was following her out of the room when his eye
was caught by the heap of photographs in the fireplace.
Photographs . . .   People paid money for photographs.
William didn't see very well how he could reduce those
photographs into the cash that presumably they
represented, but it seemed a pity to leave good saleable
articles lying about to be destroyed.   He gathered
them up, took them into his bedroom, hid them in a
drawer, and forgot all about them.

He met the Outlaws the next day.   Their search for

the money for their entrance fees had been as fruitless as his.

"I even asked for it for my next Christmas present," said Ginger gloomily. "Told 'em they could knock it off whatever they were goin' to buy me next Christmas an' they wouldn't . . . Well, I simply can't understand 'em. I know that if I'd got all the money they seem to have I wouldn't mind givin' two shillings to people what needed it as much as I do."

"That's what I said to 'em," said Douglas. "I said that they sent money to hospitals an' why cun't they give me a bit. I told 'em that I needed it a jolly sight more than any hospital did."

"What did they say to that?" said Henry, much impressed by the irrefutability of the argument.

"They went on and on and on about all the money they spent on my clothes an' food an' school bills. Well, I said that I'd gotter have food to keep me alive so I couldn't do without food, but I *could* do without school an' I offered to stay away from school next term jus' to save them money if they'd give me two shillings of the money they saved, which wasn't much considerin' that they pay *pounds* to send us to school, an' they wouldn't even *listen* to me . . . An' of course I couldn't tell them what it was for."

"Well," said William, "we've tried asking for it, so now we've got to try getting it other ways."

"It's no use having any sort of a show," said Ginger sadly. "We didn't make any money at all the last one we had."

"The prehistoric animal one?" said Douglas.

"Yes. Don't you remember? Only four people came an' they wouldn't pay more than a halfpenny each, an' Jumble wouldn't act a Pterodactyl properly

though we'd taken *hours* teaching him how to do it,
an' they all made us give them their money back.   In
any case," he ended gloomily, "it wouldn't have been
more than twopence . . .   Well, we've got to start
trying to *earn* it.   There's only a week."

"I'm sick of earning money," said Douglas.   "You
use up all your strength chopping up pounds an'
pounds of firewood for them an' they give you a halfpenny at the end and then take it back because you've
chopped up something they didn't want chopped up or
because something's gone wrong with the axe.   Or
they promise you a halfpenny for doing an errand and
then won't give it you just because the change turns
out wrong or you've forgotten what they told you to
get.   As if one brain could hold *everything*."

"Well, anyway," said William, "we've got to *try* to
earn it.   And there's only a week so we've got to try
jolly hard."

Gloomy but determined, the Outlaws departed to
their homes.

William once more sought his mother.   He meant to
offer to clean her shoes for her for a week.   He remembered that he had once undertaken to do this in a time
of domestic crisis, and he hoped she had forgotten how
he had by mistake cleaned them with the contents of
a tin of fish paste that was meant for tea sandwiches
that day.   She had taken a great deal of trouble to get
it off, but she was still followed in the village by cats
whenever she wore that particular pair of shoes.

Ethel was with her mother in the drawing-room.
They were discussing a bazaar.   Mrs. Brown had a
passion for bazaars.   When it wasn't the Choir Fund it
was the Church Renovation Fund, and when it wasn't
that it was the Nursing Fund, and when it wasn't that

it was the Women's Guild. But it was always a bazaar. They took no notice of him, and he sat down gloomily to wait till he could get in with his shoe-cleaning offer.

"Mrs. Marlow's going to get Melchet's down in Hadley to stock a stall," Mrs. Brown was saying. "They give a third of whatever they make to the Funds. We've never had that sort of thing before, but I believe it's done quite a lot, and, of course, with the Church School bazaar only just over, people really haven't a lot of things to give to this."

Something of William's gloom fell from him.

"D'you mean," he said, "that shops can sell their things at the bazaar and give a third of the money to the bazaar and keep the rest?"

"It's done quite a lot now, dear," said Mrs. Brown absently. "I don't like it."

A light broke through William's countenance.

"D'you mean," he said, "that *anyone* could sell things there an' give the bazaar a third of the money an' keep the rest themselves."

"I suppose so," said Mrs. Brown still absently, "if they'd got anything that anyone would want to buy."

Then she seemed suddenly to awake to the fact of William's presence. "What do you want, dear?" she said.

"Nothing, thanks," said William as he disappeared through the doorway.

His Outlaws did not entirely share his optimism.

"But we've got nothing to *sell*," objected Henry. "You can't get money for *nothing*."

"We've got to *make* something to sell," said William sternly. "There's four whole days. Surely we can *make* somethin' in four days."

"Yes, but *what*?" demanded the Outlaws.

"*Tell* you what!" said William, as another bright idea struck him, "let's have it a sort of second-hand stall—what they call a White Elephant Stall." He uttered the words with contempt, remembering the acute disappointment he had suffered on first seeing the contents of the stall so misleadingly named. "Well, surely we can all find some old things we don't want."

"Yes," objected Douglas, "but most of the things I don't want no one else'd want either."

"Oh, do shut up," said William wearily. "If the great men in history had all gone on like you there wouldn't have been any great deeds done. We've got to get a stall full of things that we don't want ourselves but that other people pay lots of money for. An' we've got to have eight shillings left over when we've paid a third to the bazaar."

Even Ginger shook his head sadly at this. He knew by experience that there were times when William's optimism ran away with him.

And the result of their endeavour, as viewed in the old barn on the morning of the Sale of Work, was not encouraging.

Henry had brought a rather unsavoury pail, with half the bottom out, that he had come upon in a ditch. He said vaguely that somebody might find it useful for something.

Douglas had brought an old prayer book from which the entire Morning Service and half the Evening Service was missing, and a pair of socks that his mother had thrown away as undarnable.

Ginger had brought a bird's nest and a dead fern in a pot, which he had tied to a stick in order to keep it in an upright position, and labelled: "Rare brown Furn from the Troppiks."

William's contribution was a teapot without a spout, a razor of Robert's that had lost its blade, and a newt in a jam jar.

They gazed at the collection dispassionately.

"Well, we're not likely to get eight shillings for those," said Henry, who had spent the evening of the previous day working out the sum.

"We're likely to get a lot for that rotten old bucket you've brought," said William. "Why didn't you take a little *trouble*?"

There followed an acrimonious discussion on the rival merits of the white elephants, which was finally ended by William who said:

"Well, *talkin'* won't get us the eight shillings. I vote we all go home again and see if we can find something else."

So they all went home again to see if they could find something else. William went up to his bedroom and looked around it without much hope.

If he took any of his personal belongings, such as his soap dish or hair brush, they would be recognised and indignantly reclaimed by his mother. He opened his drawers one after the other—collars, ties, stockings. He couldn't possibly take any of them. His mother would recognise them at once. He opened the long drawer at the bottom. Ethel's photographs. He had quite forgotten them. He looked at them doubtfully. He remembered the zest with which his mother treasured all her family photographs. These men's mothers or aunts might be at the bazaar and might want to buy their photographs. It was worth trying. He gathered them together and set off briskly again to the old barn.

     *   *   *   *   *

There was a strange undercurrent of excitement in the crowded room that seemed to centre in the younger set.

Dolly Clavis, a comely damsel of about eighteen, was making her way tempestuously to the door.   Her

"THERE'S YOUR PHOTOGRAPH STANDING FOR THE WHOLE WORLD TO SEE," SAID THE OUTRAGED DAMSEL.

head was held high, her eyes were flashing angrily, her
lips set in a haughty line.   Beside her, pale and distraught, strode George (Douglas's brother).   He **was**
running his hands through his hair, then throwing them
out in passionate protest.

"I tell you it's all a mistake," he said.   "I never
admired her.   Never."

"Oh no, never," shrilled the outraged damsel sarcastically, "and there's your photograph standing for
the whole world to see with 'To Ethel from her most
humble and faithful admirer, George.' 'Her most
humble and faithful admirer, George'!" she repeated
furiously.

"I tell you it isn't me," pleaded the unhappy youth. "I tell you it's someone else who happens to have my name and a face like mine. I tell you I hate and despise Ethel Brown. It was *months* ago and I never knew she'd kept that photograph. I don't know how the hateful little wretch got hold of it. I tell you——"

"I won't listen to a word you have to say," said the lady. "Not a *word*. I'll never speak to you again. Never. Going round giving your photographs to Ethel Brown with stuff you ought to be ashamed of written all over them, and then pretending you love me!"

"I do love you," protested the youth wildly. "It was *months* ago, and I didn't mean it even at the time, and it was before I got to know you, and I tell you I hate Ethel Brown and——"

"I never want to see you or hear of you again," repeated the damsel, keeping however carefully within sight and earshot. "Go away. I hate you."

"Listen!" pleaded the youth. "Just listen——"

They had reached the door of the room. Another youth and damsel was entering it—happy, carefree, smiling fondly at each other.

The youth was Hector—Ginger's brother and George's friend. The maiden was a local belle of the name of Peggy Barton.

As the couples passed each other, George just had time to pull his friend aside and whisper wildly:

"Go and buy your photograph. Quick. There— over there by the door. Don't let her see."

Then he passed on with his offended lady love, explaining, exhorting, beseeching.

Hector gazed after them, his mouth hanging open with amazement.

"What did he say?" said Peggy.

Hector pulled himself together. "I—I don't know,"
he said. He was bewildered but uneasy. There had
been urgent secrecy in George's whisper. There had
been something disquieting in its tragic intensity.

He made his way over into the corner indicated by
George. It was rather a crowded corner, rather a
hilarious corner. He pushed his way through the
crowd. There behind a stall made by two packing-
cases joined together stood William, Ginger, Douglas
and Henry. On the packing-cases was ranged a
heterogeneous assortment of rubbish and in the front
of it a row of photographs and next to them a card
bearing the legend: "Fotografs—1d. eech."

As a matter of fact Hector did not realise that there
was a row of photographs. All he saw was his own
photograph. It was hideously large, hideously lifelike.
It seemed to fill the whole room. It was inscribed in
mountainous letters of startling blackness with the
words: "To Ethel, the most beautiful Girl in the
World, from her faithful Hector." The words seemed
not to be merely inscribed on the photograph. They
seemed to detach themselves from it and go shouting
about the room. He turned and plunged back, panic
stricken, through the crowd.

"What was there?" said Peggy. "Why didn't you
go to see?"

"I did see," said Hector smiling a ghastly smile and
mopping his brow. "There wasn't anything. I swear
there wasn't anything."

"What are people laughing at then?" said Peggy.
"I'm going to see."

"No, don't!" said Hector wildly, "don't!"

"What on earth's the matter?" said the bewildered
Peggy. "I *am* going to see."

"You mustn't," implored Hector. "Honestly you mustn't. You—you simply mustn't."

"If it's something improper," said Peggy primly, "I think it ought to be reported to the Vicar."

"It isn't anything improper," said Hector. "I swear it isn't."

"Well, I'm going to see what it is," said Peggy, plunging through the crowd. There was only one thing to be done and Hector did it. He plunged in before her, took out the first coin his fingers came upon (it happened to be a shilling), flung it at William, seized his photograph, crumpled it up, and thrust it into his pocket. When Peggy came he was standing by the packing-cases, gazing down at the photographs.

"Well," he said breathlessly but with rather a good attempt at nonchalance, "I told you there was nothing."

She gazed at the photographs, first with amazement then with suspicion (she was making sure that Hector's wasn't amongst them), then with aloof disdain.

"Why on *earth* did you want me to come and look at this?" she said coldly.

"I didn't," he said simply.

"I think it's in horribly bad taste," she said, turning away with a haughty shrug.

"So do I," said Hector, venturing to take her arm to pilot her back through the crowd.

She allowed the piloting in a way that was distinctly encouraging.

"I simply can't see what people find so attractive in Ethel Brown," she said.

Hector dug the crumpled photograph more deeply into his pocket, and skilfully intensified his activities as pilot.

"Neither do I," he said, "I never have done."

The Outlaws were surprised and bewildered by the effect of their White Elephant stall. The laughter of the bystanders at the beginning was unexpected, but grown-up laughter generally was unexpected, and the Outlaws had learnt to ignore it. The sudden appearance of Dolly Clavis, however, engaged in angry denunciation of Ginger's brother, who was escorting her, was thrilling and quite inexplicable. She pointed with eloquent gestures to the White Elephant Stall and asked George passionately why he hadn't told her from the beginning that he loved another and was only playing with her. The Outlaws concluded that she had suddenly gone mad. It seemed the only possible explanation. They were still more surprised when Hector pushed his way to the stall and with an expression of frozen horror on his face flung a shilling at them, seized his photograph and disappeared. Very thoughtfully William took his notice and altered one penny to one shilling. Evidently the market value of old photographs was higher than he had supposed.

In the distance he saw Hector stop and whisper to Jameson Jameson who was escorting Marion Dexter, another youthful belle. The smile dropped from Jameson Jameson's face like something being wiped off a slate, and, as if galvanised suddenly by some electric shock, he shot through the crowd to the Outlaws' stall, leaving his attendant nymph gazing around with bewilderment. Baring his teeth in fury at the Outlaws he flung them the first coin his fingers found in his pocket (a two-shilling piece), seized his photograph and tore it up, thrust the pieces into his pocket and shot back to the bewildered Marion. William could see him in the distance smiling a fixed and ghastly smile as he explained to her that he thought he saw someone fainting and had gone to see if he could help.

The next surprise for the Outlaws was provided by Glory Tomkins, a damsel of about nineteen. She strolled up to the White Elephant Stall and gazed at it, smiling a smile of superior amusement. Suddenly her eyes fell upon the photograph of Marmaduke Morency inscribed with the words: "To Ethel the Only Girl in the World for Marmaduke." It so happened that on Glory's mantelpiece at home stood an identical photograph with an identical inscription except that for 'Ethel' was substituted the name 'Glory.' Glory's blue eyes bulged, her rosebud mouth opened wide, then tightened ominously. She gave a low cry of rage turned on her heel and set out in quest of Marmaduke. She found him looking for her, an innocent smile on his lips, regardless of his doom.

She seized him by the arm and drew him to the White Elephant Stall. She pointed to his photograph with a gesture eloquent of anger, scorn and grief. He seized it and tore it up, ignoring the notice that advertised its price. She had turned on her heel and departed, but not too quickly. He caught her up before she reached the door. It took three hours, four boxes of chocolates from the Confectionery Stall, a large bunch of expensive flowers from the Flower Stall, a bottle of scent from the Fancy Stall, to convince her that he had never really loved Ethel and that she was to him the only girl in the world. And even then she continued to refer to the matter. News of the stall spread swiftly and urgently among the youthful males of the neighbourhood, most of whom had passed through the Ethel stage of calf love. They came in a furtive stream to the White Elephant Stall to buy back their photographs, exhibiting signs of scorn and anger, but obviously nervous and never waiting for change. It was perhaps a good thing that Ethel had decided to play truant from the Sale of Work, and go for a walk with Jimmie Moore, intending just to look in on it on her way home.

It wasn't till the last photograph had been sold that Authority suddenly realised that there was an un-authorised entertainment going on in the room. Authority had till now been so busy at the Produce Stall and the Household Stall and the Toilet Stall and the Fancy Stall and the Flower Stall and the Con-fectionery Stall, and the crowd was so thick around these stalls, that it was not at first officially noticed that the crowd was thicker in one withdrawn corner of the room than anywhere else. Nor was Authority aware of the excitement that spread like wildfire among the young beaux of the neighbourhood. Authority of course had never given its photograph to Ethel. It had contented itself with finding occasion for con-versation with her and lending her the novels of Dickens and Sir Walter Scott. But Authority, mount-ing upon a ladder in order to restore the symmetry of the festooning of the Fancy Stall (the drawing-pins that were supposed to hold it up having responded to the force of gravity), and casting a commanding eye round the room, spied the four Outlaws behind their two packing-cases of White Elephants. Authority hastily descended from the ladder in order to investigate the situation. The crowd melted away to let Authority pass. The last of the photographs had just been sold. A pale and distraught youth was scattering its frag-ments to the winds of heaven and swearing never again to commit his features to memory on photographic plate. His inamorata, who by an unkind stroke of fate had found her way to the White Elephant Stall before him, had gone home after an outburst of inspired invective in which she had told him that he was a heartless brute, that she had hated him from the moment she first set eyes on him, that he had cast her aside like an old glove, and that he could *have* Ethel Brown. He had no doubt at all of being able ultimately to melt her, but he knew by experience that it would be a long and expensive process.

Authority found the four Outlaws entrenched behind two packing-cases containing an old pail, a ragged prayer book, a bird's nest, an old pair of socks, a broken teapot, a dead fern, a bladeless razor and a newt, waiting hopefully for purchasers. After all, as William said, if people would buy old photographs there wasn't any reason why they shouldn't buy old pails and prayer books and socks.

"What's all this?" said Authority severely.

"It's a White Elephant Stall," explained William coldly, "if you want to buy anything, you can buy it, and if you don't you'd better go away and stop taking up room."

"Who gave you permission to have this stall?" said Authority, looking with stern contempt at their not very impressive array of White Elephants.

"No one," said William. "Anyone can have a stall if they give one third of the money to the Bazaar."

"I never heard such nonsense," said Authority. "Clear out at once."

William looked for a moment as if about to dispute this order, then realised that he was growing very bored with his White Elephant Stall, and that on the whole, thanks to the boom in second-hand photographs, it had done as well as was necessary. With slow dignity he collected the remains of his white elephants and departed with his Outlaws. Outside the building they counted their money. It exceeded their wildest hopes.

"*Crumbs!*" said William. "It'll pay **our** entrance fees and *more*! And all with old photographs!"

They counted out a third of it, and William took it to his mother, who was at the Fancy Stall engaged in trying to persuade an old lady who had no telephone to buy a telephone cover.

"What's that, dear?" she said absently, when William poured a little heap of coins into her hand.

"It's a third," said William.

"A what, dear?" she said.

"A third," repeated William. "A third of our stall."

"What stall, dear?" said Mrs. Brown.

"White Elephant Stall," said William.

"But you hadn't got a White Elephant Stall," said Mrs. Brown.

"Yes, we had," said William, "and that's a third."

"William," said Mrs. Brown vaguely apprehensive, "you haven't been in any mischief, have you?"

"Me," said William indignantly, "of course not."

Mrs. Brown had no time to investigate further. The old lady was obviously beginning to doubt the usefulness of a telephone cover to a telephoneless household. Mrs. Brown poured William's coins into the cash box, hoping that it was all right, and turned to the old lady.

"It would make," she said, "a very pretty tea cosy

with only a very little alteration. Or," vaguely, "you could keep things in it."

As William passed out of the room he met Ethel and Jimmie Moore just coming into it.

*　　*　　*　　*　　*

The Outlaws, in a state of eager excitement, stood at the point of the road at which they had met the tramp. Each held his two shillings in his hand. Their eyes were fixed on the point at which the gaily swaggering figure with its fluttering rags should appear.

"S'pose he doesn't come," said Ginger.

"I *bet* he'll come," said William.

"I'm going to start the *day* I'm twenty-one," said Douglas.

"Will they give us old clothes?" said Henry. "Or shall we just have to wait till ours get old?"

"I'm goin' to have a hat just like his without a top," said William.

"And eat bread and cheese with an old pen-knife," added Ginger with a blissful smile.

"And go about in woods and fields all day without having to keep tidy and come home to meals."

"And stay up as long as you like and no one bothering how dirty you get."

"He's a bit late," said Douglas anxiously.

"Well, he's a sort of King of the tramps," said Henry. "I expect he's jolly busy. Prob'ly they've got some sort of a Parliament on, and he's got to open it or something."

At that moment the gaily swaggering figure appeared at the end of the road and waved to them in friendly greeting. They ran towards it excitedly. There was a pleased smile on the gentleman's sandy countenance.

He had evidently not been quite sure of finding them there.

"Well this is splendid," he said. "Got your money?"

"Yes," said William making himself the spokesman. "Yes. We've got the money all right. Have you got the address?"

With impressive dignity the sandy gentleman took a grimy envelope out of his pocket.

"You must promise," he said, "not to open this till three minutes after I've gone and," he added still more impressively, "you must never show anyone what's inside it."

Thrilling from head to foot with excitement, the Outlaws promised.

"Well, now let's have your money," said the sandy gentleman. His eyes were glistening thirstily. "Half a crown each, wasn't it?"

"No, two shillings," said William.

"Oh yes, I forgot. Two shillings."

The Outlaws held out grimy hands in each of which reposed two very warm shillings.

But just as they did so something else happened. Round the bend in the road came a policeman, and, the minute he appeared, the tramp seemed suddenly and miraculously to vanish. They saw him for a second in the distance, his rags fluttering in the wind. A moment later he had completely disappeared.

The policeman, who was rather stout, pursued him for a short distance conscientiously if ineffectively, then returned to the Outlaws, mopping his brow.

"Tryin' to get money out of you, was he?" he said.

"We were paying him our entrance fee," said William with dignity.

"Trust him to get money out of anyone," said the policeman. "Soon as I saw him round here I knew he was up to no good."

"Do you know him?" said William.

"Should think I do," said the policeman. "We all know Sandy Dick. He's got money out of police headquarters pretending to be a Scotland Yard man on a job. He's got money out of a bishop pretending to be a converted cannibal. He can get money out of *anyone*. I suppose he was getting it out of you?"

"He's left the address anyway," said William picking up the envelope which the tramp had dropped at the policeman's appearance.

Eagerly he tore it open. There was nothing inside it.

"What did you think there'd be inside?" said the policeman.

They told him the whole story.

He put back his head and roared with laughter. With the roars of his laughter eddying around them, the Outlaws tried to see the affair as they had seen it a few minutes ago—tried and failed. The flight of their "chief," the empty envelope, the policeman's raucous and rather tactless merriment, stripped the exploit of its glamour and revealed them to themselves as inglorious dupes. But, inglorious as the affair might be, it had its redeeming features. It would have been much worse if the policeman had appeared after they had yielded up their "entrance fee," instead of just before.

They looked at their combined eight shillings with rising spirits.

"Well, my lads," said the policeman with a grin, "you'll be wiser next time."

"You're not going to put him in prison, are you?" said Henry rather anxiously.

"'Im?" said the policeman. "Sandy Dick? 'E'll be at Newcastle by now. You never knew such a sprinter. By the time you think you've got him nicely copped in Land's End you suddenly find 'e's in John o' Groats. That's the sort of chap *'e* is. You should see 'im play the toff too when 'e likes. Pass as a duke any day, 'e could."

The spirits of the Outlaws rose still higher. They had been duped by no common rogue. It was, after all, rather an honour to have been taken in by Sandy Dick.

The policeman had adjusted his helmet and belt and set off down the road.

The Outlaws stood and surveyed the wealth that was left so unexpectedly on their hands.

"Come on," said William, "I'm jolly hungry. Let's go'n' buy some lemonade and cream blodges."

The Outlaws walked down to the village with a carefree nonchalant swagger that was partly a copy of Sandy Dick's and partly expressive of their feelings. Eight shillings are eight shillings, and a feast of lemonade and cream blodges in the hand is after all worth any amount of glorious careers in the bush.

* * * * *

In the woods Ethel walked with her chosen swain. "Jimmie," she said thoughtfully, "do you remember the sale of work yesterday?"

"Yes, darling," said Jimmie.

"Well, didn't you notice," said Ethel still more thoughtfully, "that people looked at me in a *funny* way?"

"What sort of a funny way?" said Jimmie.

"I don't know. Just a *funny* way."

"What sort of people?"

"Oh, George and Hector and Jameson and Marmaduke and people like that."

"I didn't notice," said Jimmie, "but I'll go and push all their faces in for them if you like.   No trouble at all.   I'd enjoy doing it."

"Oh no," said Ethel, "it wasn't that sort of a look. It was—well, I simply can't describe it.   It was just *funny*."

"Well don't talk about them," said Jimmie, "it's a waste of breath.   Let's forget them and talk about ourselves."

So they forgot them and talked about themselves.

*   *   *   *   *

The Outlaws sat round the marble-topped table in the village confectioner's.   At each place was a glass of lemonade and in the middle of the table a large dish (already twice replenished) of cream blodges.

It was not often that the Outlaws could feast off such dainties *ad nauseam*.   To-day they could.   It was a strange and glorious feeling to be able to eat cream blodge after cream blodge without having to keep an anxious eye on the penny that each represented. The Outlaws did not in fact remember ever having had such riches at their disposal before.

"We can buy some new fishing nets after this," said Ginger.   "Ours are full of holes."

"And some more marbles," said Douglas.

"And *lots* of sweets," said Henry.

"You know I never thought we'd make half so much money by the White Elephant Stall," said William.

"It was the photographs that people paid so much for," said Ginger.

"Yes," said Douglas, "and the funny thing was

they all bought their own photographs. I thought it
would be their mothers or aunts who'd buy them."

"Yes, I thought it was jolly conceited of them,"
said William, "they seemed jolly bad tempered about
it, too. It was all," he said reflectively, "a bit queer,
somehow."

"Yes, but it's been all right for us," said Ginger.

The Outlaws dismissed the slightly puzzling element
that there had undoubtedly been about the affair, and,
ordering another dish of cream blodges and four more
bottles of lemonade, surrendered themselves to the
cheering reflection that it had been all right for them.

CHAPTER IX

WILLIAM AND THE SLEEPING MAJOR

THE Outlaws were wandering through the wood, discussing what to do with the afternoon that, full of glorious possibilities, lay before them.

"Let's try'n' make up some game we've never played before," said Ginger.

"Yes," said Henry. "Let's——"

He stopped.

They had reached a bend in the path and there, just in front of them, by the side of the path, was an elderly man of military appearance who was fast asleep in a bath chair with the remains of a picnic around him.

At first the Outlaws approached very carefully, lest any unguarded movement should rouse the sleeping warrior to wakefulness and wrath. Gradually, however, they grew bolder, and began to approach with less caution. Finally they stood round his chair. He had not even stirred in his sleep.

"He's dead," said Ginger cheerfully.

"He can't be," said Douglas. "He's breathin'."

"P'raps he's dyin'," said Ginger still more cheerfully. "P'raps if we wait a bit, he'll stop breathin'."

They stood round the bath chair, watching and waiting expectantly, but the deep breathing still continued.

"He's not dyin'," said Ginger, disappointedly.

William cleared his voice and said, "Hi!" in a voice only slightly louder than Ginger's.

At this moment a wasp stung Douglas, and he uttered a loud yell. The Outlaws turned and fled precipitately from the scene. When they had fled for some distance, however, it occurred to them that they were not being pursued. They stopped and looked back. The elderly gentleman was still slumbering peacefully in his bath chair. Very cautiously, in fear of a ruse, they returned. But there was no ruse. The elderly gentleman continued to slumber peacefully. They gathered round him again, and began to make noises of various degrees of audibility, to see whether the sleeping occupant of the bath chair would show any reaction to any of them. He continued to slumber peacefully. They grew bolder.

"Boo!"

"Yah!"

"*Hoi!*"

"Вαн!"

There was a certain thrill about the proceeding. It was like baiting a lion in his den. At any minute the ferocious old gentleman might suddenly awaken and leap on them in fury. But he didn't, and at last they tired of it.

"Come on!" said Henry. "Let's go'n' play at something."

"Let's see what he's been havin'," said Ginger.

Search in the picnic basket revealed the remainder of a pork pie, and several buns, and a small empty bottle that had contained wine.

"Seems sort of waste to leave this," said William, holding up the pork pie. "It'll only get stale an' he can't eat anythin' dyin' like this. People're always

tellin' us that it's wrong to leave bits of food lyin'
about in woods after picnics an' such-like. I bet it'd
be a kindness to eat it jus' to clear it out of the way.
Well, we don' want the pore ole man to get into
trouble for it anyway."

"He won't if he dies," objected Ginger.

"Oh, shut up arguin' about it," said William, taking
a large bite out of the meat pie and handing it to
Douglas.

For the next few minutes the Outlaws were deprived
of the power of speech. It was a largish piece of meat
pie, and provided them with three bites each. The
custom of the Outlaws when sharing anything in the
nature of a pork pie was to take a bite in turns till the
thing was finished. By dint of long practice, their
mouths had acquired the knack of accommodating, as
a "bite," a portion of the whole that would have
staggered an ordinary adult. Occasionally, of course,
one of them overreached himself. The mouth had to
be able to close completely over the mouthful or it did
not count and the next turn had to be missed. The
consumption of the meat pie and cakes occupied them
for the next few minutes. Then Ginger approached
the sleeping warrior.

"He's not dead yet," he announced, speaking in a
muffled voice. "He's still breathin'."

"I don' think he's goin' to die," said Douglas. "I
don' think he'd look as red as that. Not if he was
goin' to die. He'd look pale. Dyin' people always
look pale."

"Oh, well," said William, who was losing interest
in the question, "p'raps he isn't. It's jus' possible
that he isn't. He may've got some sort of illness
where you go on sleepin' for the rest of your life an'

never wake up. I've heard of illnesses like that. You go on sleepin' for the rest of your life an' never wake up."

"I bet I wouldn't mind an illness like that," said Ginger wistfully. "You'd never have to go to school or church or anythin'. Better than the sort of illnesses I always get. Mumps," he ended bitterly. "Mumps, and earaches an' things like that."

"Oh, come on," said Douglas. "Let's go an' play at somethin'."

"Yes, let's," said Henry, "this is a trespass wood, too. You know how mad they were last time they found us in it. Let's get out of it quick."

"Well *he's* not got no right to be in it either," said William, who was obviously unwilling to abandon his find. "I don' think we ought to leave him in here where he's got no right any more than we have. We oughtn't to leave a pore ole man like this to be gone on at by that keeper the way he goes on at us. Well, I'm not goin' to go away an' leave him. I'm going to take him along with me."

The Outlaws made no serious objection. To the other three as to William it seemed rather tame to go away, leaving their strange and intriguing find behind them.

It was a breathless moment when William laid his hands upon the handle of the bath chair, and began cautiously to propel it along the path. His tongue was extended to its full length in the stress of the moment, his eyes were fixed warily upon the nodding head, his whole body poised for flight. But the breathless moment passed. The nodding head continued to nod. The eyes in the fiery face remained closed. The band began to breathe freely again, began even to raise their voices as they discussed the situation together.

"If he died sudden now," said Ginger importantly, "there'd be a ninquest an' we'd have to go to it."

"What's a ninquest?" said William suspiciously.

"Whenever anyone dies sudden," said Ginger, "they have a ninquest to find out why they're dead, and the ones that were with them when they died have to go to it. And then if anyone's killed him they catch 'em that way. He has to go to it an' so they catch him there."

"I say," said William excitedly, pointing to his cargo, "let's have a ninquest on him."

"We can't," said Henry. "He's still breathin'."

"That doesn't matter," said William impatiently; "we can pretend he's dead, can't we? He's as near dead as anyone could be—not movin' an' with his eyes closed. The only difference is that he's breathin' an' that's not much. Yes, let's have a ninquest on him. I'll be the judge."

"It isn't a judge when it's a ninquest," said Ginger importantly.

"What is it, then?" challenged William.

Ginger, frowning deeply, pursued an elusive word in his mind for a minute before replying.

"It's a—a coronationer."

"A what?" said William.

"A coronationer," said Ginger a little more firmly, seeing that William was merely challenging his statement for form's sake and not at all because he disbelieved it.

"I knew he was," said William. "I was only seein' if you knew. Well, I'll be the coronationer an' you can be the murderer, an' Douglas can be the policeman an' Henry can be——" He appealed to Ginger, who had by this time established his reputation as an authority on inquests. "Who else has there got to be besides a coronationer an' a murderer an' a policeman?"

"There's always gotter be a doctor at a ninquest," said Ginger.

"All right, Henry can be the doctor," said William.

The difficulties of getting the bath chair over the stile into the field where the old barn was, proved insuperable, and so the inquest was held in a part of the road just near the stile. Fortunately it was a little-used road, so the band could conduct operations without fear of interruption. William, as coroner, sat on the fence with the sleeping warrior in the bath chair, as corpse, just in front of him. The murderer and policeman and doctor grouped themselves around the corpse. The coroner opened proceedings by saying, "Ladies, and gentlemen——" then, further invention failing him, pointed to the corpse and addressed the doctor.

"Is this man dead?"

"I should think you could see for yourself he is," said the doctor; "use your eyes, can't you?"

"You jolly well shut up talking to me like that," said the coroner indignantly, "and you ought to say 'Sir' or 'My lord' or something like that when you speak to me. And it's *your* business knowin' when people are dead, not mine. If you're a doctor you're supposed to have passed examinations in tellin' whether people are dead."

The doctor conducted a lengthy and elaborate examination of the corpse, keeping a careful distance from it.

"Yes," he pronounced, at last, "he's dead all right."

"What did he die of?" said the coroner.

The doctor conducted another examination—yet more lengthy and elaborate—keeping a still more careful distance from it.

"He's died of slow poison," he pronounced at last.

"Who poisoned him?" said the coroner.

"I did," said the murderer.

"What for?" said the coroner.

"'Cause I wanted to," said the murderer.

"All right. You'll have to be hung," said the coroner.

"I don't care," said the murderer.

The coroner turned to the policeman.

"You go an' hang him an' mind you do it properly, or you'll get hung yourself as well."

They proceeded to hang Ginger, who made a most satisfactorily recalcitrant criminal. He escaped twice, and struggled so realistically that the doctor retired from the fight half-way through to nurse a black eye, and the coroner was sent flying into a ditch.

Finally Ginger himself tired of it and allowed himself to be hanged, indulging in such realistic death struggles that William almost regretted not having chosen that rôle himself. They then returned to the gentleman in the bath chair, who was still sound asleep. William had the brilliant idea of taking a letter, which protruded slightly out of a pocket, in order to find out his name. The letter was addressed to Major Franklin.

"That's his name," explained William. "Well, I'm gettin' a bit tired of this game. I vote we go'n play Red Indians for a bit."

The others were inclined to receive this proposal favourably, but Ginger pointed to the man in the bath chair, and said: "Yes, but what about *him*? We can't jus' leave him here."

"Why not?" said William.

"Well, s'pose a motor-cycle or somethin' like that comes along an' kills him? They'll say it was our fault for leavin' him here."

At that moment Victor Jameson passed along the road with a small train of followers. Victor Jameson and the Outlaws were on friendly terms.

"I say," said William, pointing to the sleeping warrior, "would you like him?"

Victor Jameson looked at the sleeping warrior with interest.

"Who is he?" he asked.

"Dunno," said William, "but you can have him for sixpence. You can have him, chair an' all, for sixpence. It's jolly cheap."

"Who does he belong to?" said Victor.

"He belongs to us," said William; "we found him in a wood."

"Why is he asleep like that?"

"Dunno. But he's all right. He's jolly fine to play games with. He goes on sleepin' like this an' he never wakes up. Look here, you can have him *an'* his chair for fivepence halfpenny. It's a bargain."

Victor and his followers submitted the bargain to a lengthy inspection, and consulted together.

"You can pretend he's a king on a throne or someone's ole grandfather," said William. "Or if you're playin' pirates, he'd do for the ship you're attackin' or anything like that. An' he never wakes up." He paused, then said: "Fourpence halfpenny, then. It's jolly cheap."

"We'll take him," Victor finally announced to William, "if you'll let us have him for threepence."

"All right," said William, "threepence."

They handed over the threepence, and the Outlaws departed.

*   *   *   *   *

A girl and a young man stood in the clearing in the wood and looked about them desperately.

"But—but we left him here," said the girl wildly, "we left him here after lunch, he *can't* have gone away."

The young man took out his handkerchief and mopped his brow.

"What—what a ghastly thing to have happened!" he said.

"Well, *do* something about it, can't you?" snapped the girl.

"What *can* I do?" retorted the youth with spirit.

"Find him."

"I'm going to. But we've got to think out some plan of action first. I mean before we start looking for him we've got to form some sort of idea where he is, haven't we?"

"Well, where can he be?"

"I don't know. That's what we've got to try and think of."

"One of the keepers can't have turned him out of the wood, can they?"

"Of course not. They all knew that we've got permission to come in."

"He—Charlie, he can't have wakened up and found we'd gone off and left him, can he?"

"I don't see how he can."

"You—you put the sleeping-draught in his wine, didn't you?"

"Yes. It's always acted before."

"Oh, dear," moaned the girl. "It's a judgment on us. It was wrong."

"Nonsense. You know what he's like when he doesn't have it. Keeps us dancing attendance on him all the afternoon, and his temper absolutely foul. Now if I put a drop of sleeping-draught into his wine he sleeps like a lamb and wakes up as fresh as a daisy."

"Charlie, he's been kidnapped and they're holding him up to ransom!"

"Rats!"

"He'll be mad if he finds that we go off and leave him, you know. He thinks that we spend all the afternoon sitting by his bath chair reading and waiting for him to wake up for tea."

"Well, let's go down to the village and see if we can find any news of him there."

"Yes, that seems the best thing to do."

They went down to the village and the first person they met was William.

The Outlaws had had a most enjoyable game of Red Indians and had just separated to go home for tea.

"Excuse me, little boy," said the girl sweetly, "but have you seen anything of an old gentleman in a bath chair?"

William considered. So recent and vivid was his memory of the game of Red Indians that it was some time before the memory of the old gentleman in the bath chair came to him through the mists of the past. A guarded look spread over his face as the memory returned.

"Why?" he said. "Have you lost one?"

"Yes," said the girl eagerly. "My cousin and I took our uncle into the wood for a little picnic and left him there just a minute after lunch—well, not much longer than a minute, anyway—and when we came back he'd gone."

"Oh," said William, assuming an expression of surprise and concern as a cloak to the quick and anxious cogitations that were taking place in his mind. "Have —have you looked for him in the wood?"

"Yes," said the girl, "at least we looked just near the place we left him. It was one of his gouty days, you see. He couldn't walk any distance at all. Have —have you seen anything of an old gentleman in a bath chair?"

The young lady had blue eyes and a winning manner and William was anxious to help her, but it was a situation requiring delicate handling. He assumed the expression of one who is thinking deeply, and then of one to whom some distant but illuminating memory has just returned. Both expressions were quite well done.

"Wait a minute," he said, "I think I remember a boy tellin' me he'd seen an ole gentleman in a bath chair."

"Oh, do tell us where he lives," said the girl, "and we'll go and ask him."

"No, I'll ask him," said William kindly, "don' you bother askin' him. I know him, you see, an' so I'd better ask him. He might remember it better with me askin' him."

"It's most *awfully* kind of you," said the girl gratefully.

"Oh, that's quite all right," said William, "that's quite all right. I like helpin' people."

He led them down the road to Victor Jameson's house and looked anxiously about. There were no signs of the old gentleman in his bath chair.

"You'd better stay out here in the road," he said to the man and girl, "'cause—'cause," with a sudden flash of inspiration, "'cause they've got a very savage dog. It knows me, but anyone it doesn't know it goes for something terrible."

His new friends seemed impressed by this argument. He hoped they would catch no glimpse of the friendly puppy who was the Jamesons' sole canine staff. They stood in the road outside the gate while he made his cautious way round to the back of the house. There he uttered the low whistle which took the place of his visiting-card. All his friends and acquaintances knew it. At once Victor emerged (also cautiously, for visits from William were not encouraged by his parents) from the side door.

"I say," said William in a hoarse whisper, "where's that ole man we sold you? They're lookin' for him. I'll buy him back for twopence. You've had him all the afternoon an' you can't expect to get as much for him as you paid for him after havin' him all afternoon."

"We've not got him," said Victor, "we played with him for a bit an' then we got tired of him—you can't play many games with him, you know—so we sold him to the Badlow twins. They wanted him for a tunnel to their train. They've got a new train an' they wanted to make it go under his chair for a tunnel so we said they couldn't 'less they bought him, so they bought him."

"How much did they pay for him?" said William.

"Twopence."

"All right," said William, "I'll go an' buy him back off them an' they'll have to take a penny for him. They can't have more than a penny for him if they only paid twopence an've had him all afternoon."

He returned slowly and thoughtfully to the waiting couple. The girl was standing at a safe distance from the gate, watching it fearfully, obviously prepared every moment for the sally of a ferocious hound.

"This," said William, fixing them both with his most expressionless regard, "this isn't the *acshul* boy what saw him. He says that what he meant wasn't that he'd *acshully* seen him but that he'd seen someone what'd said he'd seen him."

"Did he tell you who it was?" said the girl.

"Yes," said William, "I'll go with you to him now."

"It's really very kind of you," said the young man gratefully.

"Oh, no," said William. "It's quite all right. I like helpin' people."

He led them in silence down the road to the house where the Badlows lived. He felt relieved by the news that it was the Badlow twins who had bought the bath chair and its occupant. Though of great physical strength and wickedness for their age, the twins were only four years old. It ought to be quite easy to force them to surrender their purchase and to invent some explanation for its disappearance from the wood. The Badlow twins might easily have mistaken the old man for their grandfather, to whom the old man probably bore a striking likeness, and, finding him in the wood, had been inspired by filial devotion to bring him home. They had probably only just realised their mistake. William's spirits rose as he walked round to the back of the Badlows' house. But they sank when he saw the bath chair standing in the back yard without its occupant.

He uttered his whistle and the twins' elder brother, a harassed-looking boy of William's age, but of ex-

emplary character, appeared at the side door. Owing
to his exemplary character, he was not a very intimate
friend of William, but there was no actual hostility
between them.

William pointed to the tenantless bath chair.

"Where is he?" he gasped.

"Who?" said the brother.

"The man that was in that."

"That? The twins have been playing with that.
They've been using it for a tunnel for their train."

"Y-yes, but where's the man that was in it?"

The twins' brother looked at the chair without much
interest.

"Was there a man in it?" he said.

"Yes," stammered William. The whole thing was
beginning to assume the proportions of a nightmare.
"There was a man in it asleep."

"P'raps he woke up an' got out."

"No," said William, "he couldn't have done. He'd
got a sort of sleeping disease. He can't wake up. Not
possibly he can't. We'd tried. Where are they,
anyway?"

"The twins?"

"Yes,"

"Mother's taken them into Hadley to get some new
shoes."

"When will they be back?"

"Not till bed time. They're going to tea with an
aunt when they've got their shoes."

"*Crumbs!*" said William desperately.

"What's the matter?"

"Din'—din' they say *anything* about an ole man?"

"Wait a minute," said the twins' brother slowly.
"Yes, they did, too. I remember now one of 'em said,

'Narsy ole man in it. Din' want him. Frew 'im away.' I remember now. John said that. He said: 'Narsy ole man in it. Din' want him. Frew him away.'"

"ANYWAY," SAID THE YOUNG MAN, "THANKS AWFULLY FOR TRYING TO HELP US."

"*Golly!*" gasped William. "Did he say where he'd thrown him away?"

"No. He just said that. I didn't take much notice when he said it, but now I remember. He said that."

"An' he din't say any more than that?"
"No."
"An' they won't be back till bed time?"
"No."

**WILLIAM HELD OUT A HAND FOR THE HALF-
CROWN AND POCKETED IT GRATEFULLY.**

"Crumbs. It's one of the awfullest things that's
ever happened to me, losing an ole man like this. It's
all Victor's fault for selling him to them."

"What is?" said the twins' brother innocently.

But William was walking slowly back to his friends.

"Well?" they said anxiously.

"I—I'm afraid that it was a mistake," said William faintly. "I—I'm afraid that it was this boy's brother an' that they only *thought* they saw a man in a bath chair, but they weren't sure."

"Anyway," said the girl, "it mightn't have been the same man."

"No," said William, brightening, "I don't think it was."

"And, anyway," said the young man, "thanks awfully for trying to help us."

William held out a hand for the half-crown and pocketed it gratefully.

Just opposite the Badlows' gate where they were standing was the entrance to a farm and the farmer was just now coming down the road to it. Like most farmers of the district he cherished no great love for William and his band.

He glanced coldly and suspiciously at William, then turned beaming expansively upon his companions.

"G'd afternoon, Mr. Charles," he said, "how's the major?"

"He's—he's——" began the unhappy Charles and ended abruptly. "You haven't seen him this afternoon by any chance, have you?"

"No, but he was looking fine last time I seed him. I were just thinkin' of you, Mr. Charles," he went on. "I want to show you my Henrietta. You remember me showin' you her when she was a little one. Her's fine, now. You did ought to see her. Her's just in here."

He swept them all into his farmyard. He didn't actually invite William. In fact, the look he cast on William was the reverse of inviting. But William could not resist the temptation entering the farmyard thus under the shield of an invitation that might be supposed to include himself, nor could he endure to leave the adventure in this incomplete state.

The first sight that met their eyes was that of Henrietta fraternising with some hens and a goat in the middle of the farmyard. Henrietta was a pig of enormous proportions. The farmer looked at her in surprise.

"Well, I'll be blessed," he said, scratching his head, "how the blazes did she get out? I left her in her sty."

He opened an immaculate pigsty and invited Henrietta into it. Henrietta entered. They all leant over the low wall—the farmer, the young man, the girl, and William—while the farmer pointed out the excellences of Henrietta to them with his stick. Henrietta, becoming suddenly shy, disappeared into her sleeping quarters.

"Her's as fine a hannimal," pronounced the farmer as she departed, "as you'd find anywheres. You——"
He stopped. Strange sounds were coming from Henrietta's sleeping quarters. They listened in silence, open-mouthed. The sounds were the sounds of some-one slowly awakening and awakening to wrath.

"What the——? Who the——? Where the——? confound you, sir. What do you mean by it? Where are your manners, sir? Where were you brought up? Where were you educated? I say you're drunk, sir, you're drunk. Are you aware, sir, that you're standing on me? *Standing* on me, sir. Get off me, sir, or I'll call the police. You—Good heavens! Where am I? Where am I? Who are you, sir? Good gracious! You're a pig, a pig, sir. Did you know you were a pig, sir? A——"

"WHAT IS THE MEANING OF THIS OUTRAGE?"
THUNDERED THE MAJOR.

Slowly, upon his hands and knees, the major emerged before their horrified gaze, followed by the mildly curious Henrietta. Slowly he rose to his feet.

"What," he thundered, "is the meaning of this outrage?"

"I WILL LEAVE NO STONE UNTURNED TILL I HAVE SIFTED
THIS MATTER TO THE CORE, SIR," SAID THE YOUNG MAN.

His question was addressed impartially to the young
man, the girl, the farmer, William, and Henrietta.

The young man, feeling that the answer to the
question devolved upon him, raised a hand to his brow
and said faintly:

"I will leave no stone unturned till I have sifted
this matter to the core, sir. You may safely leave it
in my hands."

"In your hands?" roared the major. "I left
myself in your hands and this is where I find myself.
In a pigsty. *A pigsty*, sir. With a pig standing on
me. *Standing* on me. A *pig*, sir. *Literally* a pig.
How do you account for it? That's what I want to
know."

"I—I don't account for it, sir," said the young man

still more faintly. "I'm—I'm as mystified as you are."

"*Mystified!*" bellowed the major. "So you call yourself *mystified*, sir. It takes more than a word like mystified to express my feelings, sir." He then proceeded to express his feelings fairly adequately.

William felt that at this point he should have quietly disappeared. He had seen at once what had happened. The terrible twins had disposed of their encumbrance by the simple expedient of tipping him out of sight into Henrietta's sleeping quarters, releasing Henrietta in the process. But he could not tear himself away. The situation was far too absorbing.

The major, having adequately expressed his feelings and having more than adequately expressed his opinion of the young man, the girl, the farmer, William and Henrietta, remembered suddenly that it was one of his gouty days, stopped striding to and fro in the pigsty and began to limp. Then he fastened a terrifying eye upon the farmer.

"Open that gate, sir," he yelled, "and let me out."

The farmer, trembling, opened the door and the major limped out.

"I shall never get over this—never," he bellowed furiously. "Where's my chair? I say, where's my chair? Shock to my system—never get over it. I tell you sir, I feel more like riding in a hearse than a chair."

They had followed him out into the road and there stood his chair. The twins' brother, having surmised that they wanted the chair as well as the occupant, and being a conscientious youth, had kindly brought it across the road and left it for them outside the farm gate.

The young man spoke with unexpected decision.

"I can only repeat, sir," he said, "that I shall not rest till I have sifted this matter to the core."

He turned to look for William. But William had disappeared. There was a determined look in the young man's eye and William had wisely decided to make sure of having spent his half-crown before Fate should compel him to play the part of core to the young man's sifting.

CHAPTER X

WILLIAM AND THE SNOWMAN

THE Christmas holidays had begun, and, when William and his Outlaws met in the Old Barn to discuss how the four weeks should be spent, it seemed to them that the whole world and the whole of Eternity lay before them.

"If only it'd *snow*," said Ginger. "It's *years* since it snowed. Well, I know for a fact that it's years, because I remember when last it snowed I was quite young. In all the books you read it snows at Christmas, but it never seems to in real life."

"We had a jolly good time last holidays," said Douglas vaguely.

"We'd got Brent House last holidays," William reminded him mournfully.

Their last holidays had consisted of a glorious possession of an empty house and garden. The agent in whose hands it was lived in the next town, and never visited it, and people in general didn't seem to care whether the Outlaws took possession of it or not. Indeed people in general seemed to prefer that the Outlaws should take possession of it. People's attitude in general appeared to be that if the Outlaws were there they could not be anywhere else, which, held the general attitude, was all to the good. So, in the character of pirates, Red Indians, and shipwrecked mariners, the Outlaws played havoc in the garden of

Brent House. Their Red Indian camp was pitched on the rose bed, and whatever fruit they found in the kitchen garden they consumed in their characters of shipwrecked mariners, or cannibal chiefs. The trees were ships in which as pirates the Outlaws attacked each other with all the ruthlessness of internecine warfare. They found their way into the house without much difficulty, and there devised a new game, in which a gang of criminals (Ginger and William) and a gang of Scotland Yard men (Douglas and Henry) pursued each other furiously up and down stairs and held deadly hand-to-hand struggles wherever they happened to meet.

One particularly ferocious struggle took place on the landing and the four of them, still fighting wildly, rolled down the stairs in a confused heap. It was during this episode that one of the bannisters got broken. None of them could account for the breaking of the landing window, though they remembered quite plainly that it was when the house was a fortress in which William was besieged by a hostile army of Douglas and Henry, and Ginger, as the relieving force, had thrown apples up to him, that most of the bedroom windows got broken.

Even the Outlaws, who looked at their misdeeds through the rosiest of rose-coloured spectacles, realised that their tenancy had not actually improved the property, though they had taken possession of it with the firmest intentions of preserving what newspapers call its amenities. In fact William had said that their occupation of it was a kindness to its owner.

"We can't possibly do it any harm," he had said, "an' we'll keep it aired for him with breathin' in it."

It wasn't till they heard that the property was

H

sold that they stood back, as it were, and surveyed their handiwork. The result was depressing. Even William, that hardy optimist, felt apprehensive qualms.

"Crumbs!" he said. "I didn't know—I say, who broke the greenhouse roof like that?"

"You did," said Ginger, "falling out of the pear tree."

"I bet I never did! Well, p'raps I did. Any way it was you that dug that hole in the lawn."

"Well, I was lookin' for hidden treasure. And it was you that broke the top off the sundial."

"Well, I was tryin' to find how it worked. And there aren't any works in it so it must've been broke anyway. An' it was you that broke the garden seat tryin' to make a boat out of it."

But they realised that they were all equally involved, and that the best thing was to hasten from the scene as quickly as possible before any responsible person came to examine the property.

They went to a spot at the other end of the village, and played the mildest games they could think of for a whole day (they even descended to Blind Man's Buff) in the hope of persuading people that they had been playing those games on that spot all the holidays.

Rumours reached them about the new occupants of their paradise. The owner was elderly and extremely irritable, and his niece, who was to keep house for him, was young and extremely beautiful. It was Robert who unwittingly told William that the niece was young and extremely beautiful. Robert's latest "affair" had been terminated by the removal of the goddess and her family from the neighbourhood, and to Robert life without a goddess was simply not worth living. After one glance at the newcomer he had decided that she was worthy to be raised to the unoccupied pedestal, and so ingenuous was he that within five minutes of the decision the whole family knew of it.

"Sickening!" muttered William fiercely to his Outlaws. "Well, all I hope is that if ever I begin to go red whenever anyone says a girl's name someone'll stick a knife in me."

"I will," promised Ginger obligingly.

William had, of course, ample reason for disliking this new affair of Robert's. He wanted as little friendship between his family and the new tenant of Brent House as possible. He had heard that the new tenant was most indignant at the state in which he had found his property. He was reported to have said that the whole Zoo might have been let loose on it. After searching inquiries in the neighbourhood, however, he had narrowed down the "whole Zoo" to the Outlaws with William as their head, and he had promptly gone to see William's father to insist that justice should be done on William. William's father, with what William considered unnecessary officiousness, listened sympathetically to him, and did justice on William. William persisted that Robert had betrayed him to the goddess, who in her turn had betrayed him to her uncle, who in his turn had betrayed him to his father. Robert said scornfully that he didn't take enough interest in his silly affairs to talk about them to anyone, but he was glad that he'd got his deserts for once, and as far as he was concerned he only wished he'd got twice as much.

Robert had reasons of his own for feeling bitter. His affair with the new goddess was not running smoothly. Colonel Fortescue, the uncle, was putting every possible obstacle in its way, and for that Robert in his turn, blamed William.

"I don't blame him," he said, meaning the Colonel not William. "I'd feel the same if I was in his place. I'd feel I'd rather be put to death by torture than have anyone that belonged to me marrying into a family that had William in it. I can hardly count the number of times that boy's utterly messed up my life."

The goddess—whose name was Eleanor—opposed this view, though not from friendliness to William.

"I know he's simply awful," she said, "but it's not because of him that uncle doesn't want me to have anything to do with you. He's always the same whoever it is. Except Archie. It's because of Archie that he doesn't want me to have anything to do with anyone else."

Archie, it appeared, was the only son of an old friend of her uncle's who had once saved his life. Her uncle, despite his unromantic appearance, cherished romantic views, and thought that your only niece ought always to marry the only son of your old friend who has saved your life. Archie seconded this attitude, and the niece was maddeningly dutiful.

"It isn't that I like him better than you," she said to Robert. "I don't . . . I don't really. But uncle's always been so good to me and I like to please him."

When Robert, who always took a dramatic view of a situation, asked her if she really wanted to blast his whole life, she assured him that she didn't, but she had to *pretend* to be nice to Archie because it would hurt Uncle's feelings if she didn't.

Then Archie appeared on the scene and he turned out to be as handsome as a maiden's dream, though

Eleanor assured Robert quite fervently he wasn't hers.

Robert made praiseworthy efforts to win his way into the Colonel's good graces. Eleanor had told him that the Colonel was interested in Roman Britain, so Robert bought a book on Roman Britain and sat up far into the night, with a damp towel round his head, studying it. But he never got a chance of using it. The Colonel glared at him whenever they met with such ferocity that Robert's smile of greeting froze on his lips, and his views on Hadrian's Wall never got a chance of airing themselves. Even Eleanor passed him by without recognition when she was with the Colonel.

"I simply daren't, Robert," she explained. "Ever since he knew you'd asked me to go to a dance with you he's been furious. I simply daren't look at you. He's always like this with men because of Archie."

Robert, of course, persisted in laying all this at William's door, but William had troubles of his own and wasn't interested in Robert's.

When Colonel Fortescue and his niece were firmly and finally in possession of their property, the Outlaws discovered that they had left in it a telescope that one of Ginger's uncles had given him and that was their dearest treasure. All its vital organs were missing, but it was still—in appearance at any rate—indubitably a telescope, and the Outlaws would cheerfully have consigned all their other property to the flames rather than lose it. They held many anxious meetings to discuss their plan of action, and it was with feelings of conscious virtue that they finally decided to walk boldly and honestly up to the front door of Brent House and request the return of their treasure. They agreed to take an equal chance in this adventure by presenting themselves at the front door in a row, so that none should have any advantage by being at the back or disadvantage by being at the front.

It happened that the front doorstep was so narrow as only to accommodate two people with any comfort, and so this arrangement was more difficult than they had imagined. However, the Outlaws were not in the habit of abandoning a plan merely because it turned out to be difficult of accomplishment, and so when the housemaid opened the door she found four boys standing sideways on the narrow doorstep, holding on to each other in order to keep their positions.

"Please can we speak to Colonel Fortescue?" said William. He tried to turn his head to address her, but was wedged so tightly in between Ginger and Henry that all he could address was the back of Ginger's collar.

The housemaid stared at them for some minutes in amazement, then disappeared. She returned almost immediately.

"He says what do you want?" she said, still gazing at them open-eyed and open-mouthed.

"Please, we very kindly want our telescope," said William politely, still addressing the back of Ginger's collar. "It's in the summer-house."

The maid disappeared again but soon returned.

"He says you'd better try goin' to the summer-house the way you went before he came here," she said.

Then she shut the door firmly yet reluctantly, as if she could hardly bear to lose sight of these strange tightly-packed figures.

William stepped down, and the four of them drew a much-needed breath.

"Crumbs!" said Ginger, "I think I'd almost rather go alone to see him than stand packed up like that."

"Well, what did he mean?" said Douglas.

They had hastened out of the enemy's territory, and stood in a little group at the front gate.

"I think he meant that we could go'n' fetch it," said William. "I think that he was giving us permission to go'n' fetch it."

The others were not so sure of this, but William's optimism was proof against all their doubts.

"I'm cert'n that he meant he was givin' us permission to get it," said William. "I think he's feelin' sorry he made such a fuss to my father. I'm goin' in to get it anyway."

So William crawled through the hole in the hedge that had once been a small one but that their summer's occupation had worn to ample proportions, and, entering the lost paradise, strode boldly up to the summer-house, watched from the road by his faithful band. And then from behind the summer-house stepped out Colonel Fortescue. With a roar of fury he seized William, and, in the presence of his horror-stricken followers, executed severe corporal punishment upon his protesting and wriggling person.

William's first thought after this outrage was to put its retribution into higher hands. He thought that his father would be able to avenge it more adequately than he could.

"He'll go to the police about it," he explained to the Outlaws, "and they'll listen to him, 'cause he's grown up. They never listen to me. I've often tried goin' to them about things. I bet my father'll get him put in prison for life."

But William's father's attitude was disappointing. He merely said that he would thank Colonel Fortescue personally the next time he met him, and expressed

the wish that other householders in the district would
deal with William in the same way instead of bothering
him with complaints.

"Yes," said William bitterly, "it's just like him.
Some fathers would wipe out an insult like that with
blood. I only hope," he added darkly, "that he won't
live to be sorry."

It was in such moments as this that William summoned a picture of the future in which he was a world
potentate, and his father knelt before him and begged
for his life. This picture restored his self-respect, and
he assumed his most sinister world-potentate manner
as he continued:

"Yes, I shun't be surprised if he lives to wish he'd
done something a bit different when his only son was
insulted with a deadly insult what ought to be wiped
out with blood. At least," he added, remembering
facts, "one of his only sons, which is just the same."

That, of course, reminded him of Robert, so he went
to Robert, and pointed out to him the duty of a brother
whose only brother is brutally assaulted.

"You can go an' treat him the same as he treated
me," he said, "or you can get him put into prison.
don't mind which. But someone's gotter do something about a deadly insult like that. It oughter be
wiped out with blood."

But Robert's answer was merely a bitter laugh, and
an ironical admonition to William to try if he couldn'
mess up his life a bit more.

"Likely he'll let me *look* at her now, isn't it?" he
said, "thanks to you and your monkey tricks."

William decided to keep Robert in suspense even
longer than his father, when he was a world-potentate
and Robert came to plead for his life.

The situation had been intensified by Archie's coming to spend Christmas at Brent House. The sight of Archie walking past the house with Colonel Fortescue and the beautiful Eleanor raised Robert's resentment against Fate in general and William in particular to fever pitch.

"If I'd had anyone but you for a brother," he said, "I might have won her by now."

"And if I'd had anyone but you for a brother," retorted William as bitterly, "I wouldn't be goin' about with an insult what ought to be wiped out with blood still unavenged."

So affairs stood when the Christmas holidays began, and hence the mournfulness with which William said:

"We'd got Brent House last holidays."

It was the double mournfulness of a paradise lost and a deadly insult unavenged.

"Never mind," said Ginger, trying to lighten the general gloom of the atmosphere, "I bet it'll snow. I bet you anything that we wake up to-morrow and find it snowing."

"And I bet you anything we don't," said William, refusing to have the general gloom lightened.

But Ginger was right. They woke up the next morning to find the ground thickly covered with snow. Even William's determined mournfulness wasn't proof against that. Moreover, Robert lost his voice and developed what he called a "funny feeling," and Mrs. Brown, finding that his temperature was 101°, put him to bed and sent for the doctor.

William tried not to feel elated by this, but he couldn't help feeling that it was a judgment on Robert for refusing to avenge him, and so it was with the blithe spirit of one who sees the guilty stricken down by a just Providence that William set out to spend the afternoon with the Outlaws.

The afternoon passed quite pleasantly. After an exhilarating snowball fight which degenerated into an indiscriminate stuffing of snow down necks, and in which they all became soaked to the skin, they decided to make a snowman.

They worked hard for an hour and the result was, they considered, eminently satisfactory. The snowman was life-size, and well proportioned, and his features, marked out by small stones by William, denoted, the Outlaws considered, a striking and sinister intelligence. Having made him, they considered next what to do with him.

"Let's pretend he's a famous criminal an' have a trial of him," suggested William.

The others eagerly agreed.

William was to be the judge, Ginger counsel for the prosecution, Douglas counsel for the defence, and Henry the policeman.

They stood in a row facing him, and William addressed him in his best oratorical manner.

"You're had up for being a famous criminal," he said sternly, "and you'd better be jolly careful what you say or you'll get hung."

The snowman evidently accepted the advice, and preserved a discreet silence.

"The policeman says," went on the judge, "that you've murdered forty people an' stolen over a hundred jewels an' that he had an awful job in catching you. You oughter be ashamed of yourself, carryin' on like that. This gentleman," pointing to Ginger, "is goin' to make a speech against you, an' this gentleman," pointing to Douglas, "is goin' to make a speech for you, an' if I think you did it you're jolly well goin' to get hung."

Ginger stepped forward to address the prisoner.

"Ladies an' gentlemen," he began, then stopped and looked at the prisoner with distaste. "Couldn't we get a coat an' hat for him? He looks so silly like that. He doesn't *look* like a crim'nal. You can't imagine him goin' into shops an' places an' stealin' things all naked like that."

William accepted the suggestion with enthusiasm. "Yes," he said, "it's a jolly fine idea. . . . *Tell* you what!" he added excitedly, "I'll get Robert's coat an' hat. He's in bed with a sore throat, an' he won't know, an' anyway it's not wrong, 'cause he can't use them so someone else might as well. I'll go'n' get 'em now."

Fortunately, no one was in the hall, and he had no difficulty in abstracting Robert's hat and coat from their peg on the hat-stand. The coat was a new coat of a particularly violent check that Robert's friends rather regretted, and that Robert had bought in a desperate moment when he felt that he must do something to cut out the wretched Archie or die. Certainly when wearing the coat he was such a striking figure that anyone would have looked at him first whoever he was with, but that was all that could be said for it. The goddess's attitude to it was polite but reserved, and even Robert himself was beginning to feel a little doubtful about it. William, however, had no doubts about it at all, and draped it round the shoulders of his snowman with feelings of deep gratification. The hat he tilted slightly forward at a sinister angle over the stone eyes.

"Well," he said, with a sigh of satisfaction, "I bet

he looks as much like a crim'nal as anyone *could* look. Now go on, Ginger."

Ginger again stepped forward and began his speech.

"Ladies an' gentlemen. . . . What I've gotter say is that this man's a crim'nal, an' if anyone says he isn't I'll smack their heads for them. I watched him goin' into a jeweller's shop, an' stealin' a hundred pearl necklaces, rare an' valuable pearl necklaces, worth at least a pound each." He addressed the prisoner. "Did I or didn't I see you go into the shop an' steal a hundred rare an' valuable pearl necklaces, worth at least a pound each?" The prisoner continued silent. "You see," said Ginger triumphantly, "he can't say I didn't. . . . An' I've seen him killin' folks too. Hundreds of 'em. Shootin' 'em an' such-like. He's a murderer as well as a robber. Well"—he addressed the prisoner again—"haven't I seen you murderin' folks?" The prisoner still preserved silence. "There!" said Ginger triumphantly, "he can't say I haven't. Well, I've proved he's a murderer an' a robber an'"—to Douglas—"I don't jolly well see how you can unprove it."

"Well, I jolly well do," said Douglas. "If you saw him taking valuable pearl necklaces, why didn't you stop him? An' if you saw him shootin' folk, why din' you stop him? I don't b'lieve he did it at all. I b'lieve it was you what did it an' you're tryin' to put it on to him." He addressed the snowman. "Can you honestly say that it wasn't this man that did it?" The snowman still maintained silence. "There!" said Douglas triumphantly. "He can't honestly say it wasn't you that did it, so it *was* you that did it."

"If he didn't do it," said Ginger, "let him say he didn't do it."

"He daren't," said Douglas, "'cause you've told him that if he tells on you you'll cut his throat, but I can tell by the way he's lookin' at me that he didn't do it. He's tellin' me as plain as possible by the way he's lookin' at me that he din' do it an' you did."

"Oh, is he?" said Ginger. "I'll tell you what he's sayin' by the way he's lookin' at you. He's sayin'——"

But at this point William interrupted them with an excited exclamation of "Look!"

They looked at the path that led through the field, and there was Colonel Fortescue coming along slowly, his eyes on the ground. It was quite obvious that he had not seen them.

"Quick!" whispered William, retreating into the shelter of the wood that bordered the field. "Quick! Make snowballs for all you're worth."

He felt that at last Fate had delivered his enemy into his hands. The Outlaws worked with a will, and, by the time Colonel Fortescue had come abreast with them, they had a good store of ammunition.

"One, two, three—go!" whispered William.

The startled Colonel suddenly received—from nowhere, as it seemed to him—a small hail of snowballs. They fell on his eyes and ears, they filled his mouth, they trickled down his neck. He was blinded, deafened, winded by them. But not for long. The frenzy of the attack abated, and, as his sight and wind returned to him, he looked round furiously for the author of the outrage. Dusk was falling, but he plainly saw a figure in a coat and hat standing at the end of the field near the wood. No one else was in sight.

The snowballs had come from that direction. There wasn't the slightest doubt in the Colonel's mind that the figure in the coat and hat had thrown them. He strode across to it, trembling with rage. His rage increased as he approached. The Colonel was short-sighted, but he knew that coat. It had dogged him and haunted him in his walks with Archie and his niece. It clothed the form of the presumptuous youth who dared to try to thwart his plans for his Eleanor's happiness.

By the time he reached it his rage had passed the bounds of his self-control.

"You impudent young puppy!" he said. "How dare you . . ."

Words failed him. He raised his arm and struck out with all his might.

Now a thaw had set in soon after the Outlaws had finished the snowman, and Robert's tweed coat— which was very thick and very warm—had completed the effect. As the Colonel struck the figure, it crumpled up, and lay, an inert mass, at his feet. He gazed down at it through the dusk with eyes that started out of his head with horror, then with a low moan turned and fled from the scene of his crime.

The Outlaws crept out from behind the bush that had concealed them. William's feelings were divided between elation and apprehension.

"Crumbs, we got him all right!" he said. "I got one in his eye an' one in his ear an' two down his neck. Crumbs, wasn't it funny when he knocked the snow-man down! . . . But, I say, I'd better be gettin' Robert's hat an' coat back. Ole Colonel Fortescue'll be tellin' someone an' gettin' me into a row. . . . Let's take the snowman into the wood, too, then we can pretend we never had one here if anyone makes a fuss about Robert's coat."

They bundled up Robert's hat and coat, and rolled what was left of the snowman into the wood. Before they could make their escape, however, they saw the form of Colonel Fortescue, returning through the dusk, and hastily took shelter again behind the bushes. The gallant Colonel was not alone. Archie was with him. They both looked pale and frightened. When they reached the spot where the snowman had been, they stopped, and the Colonel looked about him on the ground, his eyes and mouth wide open with terror. Then he took out a handkerchief, and mopped his brow.

"Great heavens!" he said, "it's gone."

"What's gone?" said Archie.

"The corpse. I left it just here."

"It couldn't have gone. You couldn't have killed him."

"I did, Archie, I swear I did. I shall feel it to my dying day. He crumpled up and fell like a log. Like a log. I must have hit some vital organ. I've never killed a man before, but there was no mistaking it. It was a dead man that fell." He took out his handkerchief and mopped his brow again. "Good heavens, what shall I do?"

"You say he'd been snowballing you?"

"Yes. He'd thrown about a dozen in quick succession. I lost my temper, Archie. I'd got snow in my mouth and eyes and ears and down my neck. I went up to him, and hit out with all my strength. I must be a stronger man than I thought. He went down at my feet like a log, and lay there without a movement, and, if ever a man was dead, he was. Archie, it's the most horrible thing that ever happened to anyone. I—I don't know what to do. I merely meant to teach him a lesson. I didn't want to kill him."

"What on earth was the fellow snowballing you for?"

"Looking back on it, Archie, I think that he must have been suffering from temporary insanity. I'm short-sighted, as you know, but I did notice just before I struck the fatal blow that he looked very pale. Pale and wild-looking. I'm afraid that the poor fellow must have been out of his mind. It's—horrible to think that I killed him. I wonder—Archie, do you think a jury would consider it done in self-defence? I mean, would his snowballing count an assault?"

"You're sure it was young Brown?"

"Absolutely. I recognised his coat even before I saw his face."

"You couldn't have killed him, Uncle, or his body would have been here."

"He fell without a cry or a moan, and lay there like a log. I shall remember it to my dying day. And my dying day, Archie, may be nearer than I think!"

"But still he's not here now. He may have——"

"Crawled into the woods to die," supplied the Colonel wildly, "or crawled home. . . . If he got anywhere in time he'd tell them . . . Archie, the police may be out looking for me now. I came straight back to you, Archie, because I knew I could depend on you. I knew you'd stick by me through thick and thin."

But Archie seemed to have views of his own on that subject.

"That's all very well, Uncle," he said. "I'm—I'm frightfully sorry for you and all that, but—well, but you can't expect me to mix myself up in an affair of this sort. You've got yourself into this mess, and

I'm afraid you'll have to get yourself out of it as best you can."

"You mean you won't stand by me, Archie?" said the Colonel pathetically. "Think of—Eleanor!"

"If you're going to be tried for murder, I'm afraid that it's not much use my standing by you. Honestly, Uncle, I've got my reputation to think of. No man can afford to be mixed up in a case of this sort. Besides"—his voice rose to a frightened squeak—"how do I know that I mayn't be brought into it too? You shouldn't have brought me here, Uncle. People may say that I did it. . . ."

"What are you going to do then, Archie?"

"I'm sorry, Uncle, but I'm going straight back to pack my things, and I'm going home to-night. I'm sorry not to be able to stay over Christmas, after all, but, if things are as you say, you won't be wanting visitors. You may not even be at home to entertain them."

And the gallant Archie turned, and scuttled away through the snow to pack his things.

The Colonel turned and staggered brokenly away towards the Browns' house.

William, however, got there first. William had run home by a short cut, hung up Robert's hat and coat on the hat-stand, and slipped upstairs to Robert's bedroom to see how he was. Robert was asleep, but his mother, much touched by the proof of William's brotherly solicitude, said that the doctor had been and left him some medicine.

"I'll tell him as soon as he wakes up that you came to see how he was," she said. "He can't talk yet, of course."

William slipped downstairs and waited at the front

gate till Colonel Fortescue arrived. The Colonel stopped at the gate, looked irresolutely at the front door, then took out his handkerchief and mopped his brow.

"Robert's very very ill," volunteered William.

Colonel Fortescue gave a gasp.

"He's—he's got home?" he said.

"Oh yes," said William.

"Did he—did he crawl home?"

"I don't know," said William. "I didn't see him come home."

"Have—have they had the doctor?" gasped the unhappy Colonel.

"Oh yes," said William, "they've had the doctor."

"And—and does he think he'll live?"

"Yes," William reassured him, "he seems to think he'll live all right."

"Er—what has he told the doctor about—about what happened to him?"

"He can't speak yet," said William.

"He's unconscious?"

"Yes," said William. "I've jus' been up to his room an' he's quite unconscious."

"But you're sure they think he'll live?"

"Oh yes. They think he'll live," William reassured him.

The Colonel heaved a sigh of relief and mopped his brow again.

"It's a great relief to know that. I—I'll go home now. I'm in no fit state to interview your father or anyone just at present. I'll come round again in the morning and perhaps you'll be about to let me know how he is."

He walked on slowly down the road, and William

"DOES THE DOCTOR THINK HE'LL LIVE?" ASKED THE COLONEL.

turned three cartwheels in the middle of the road. He was enjoying his little revenge.

The next morning it happened that Robert received a letter from a friend who had been at college with him last term, but had now left to take up the study of law. He wrote to say that he was passing through the village on his motor-cycle, and would call to see Robert. Robert was much better that morning, and his voice had partly returned, so the doctor said that he might see his friend for a few minutes. The friend was with him when the Colonel arrived to find William awaiting him by the front gate. The Colonel looked as if he had passed a sleepless night.

"Well!" he whispered hoarsely, "how is he?"

"He's just a bit better this morning," said William.

"Thank Heaven!" gasped the Colonel.

"He can talk a bit this morning," said William, "he's got a lawyer up in his bedroom now."

"A lawyer!" gasped the Colonel. "He's—he's going to summon me for assault, I suppose?"

"I dunno," said William. "They're talkin' about somethin' but I dunno what."

"Better than a summons for murder," muttered the Colonel, "but terrible—terrible all the same. . . . Your father isn't in, is he?"

"No," said William, "he's gone to work."

"Yes—well, it's better perhaps to let things take their course. An apology in such a case is almost an insult. . . . I'll come round again to-morrow and you must tell me how he is."

The doctor was just coming out of the gate the next morning when the Colonel reached it. The Colonel averted his head so as not to catch the doctor's eye, and the doctor made a mental note that the old boy looked a bit queer. The old boy, in fact, looked so haggard that William—who liked to temper justice with mercy even in the case of his enemies—decided to give him a little reassurance.

"The doctor's been an' he's a lot better to-day," he said reassuringly.

"I'm glad," said the Colonel, "devoutly glad. And—and now they know the whole story from him what steps are they going to take about it?"

"They don't know anything from him," said William.

"What?" gasped the Colonel, "hasn't he told them anything?"

"No," said William, "he's not told them anything."

"You mean—they think he was just suddenly taken ill?"

"Yes," said William, "they think he was just suddenly taken ill."

"Noble fellow!" said the Colonel, evidently very much relieved. "Noble fellow! How—how different from that viper I've been cherishing in my bosom."

"You gotter viper?" said William with interest.

"Not now," said the Colonel, "I've cast him out."

"You shouldn't've done that," said William regretfully. "They're jolly rare things an' someone else might've liked it. . . . Anyway the doctor says he can come out for a little walk to-morrow if it's fine."

"Well, my boy, if you'll let me know what time he's coming out, I'd be most grateful to you. And—and I'm sorry for what happened the other day, my boy. You may come and play in my garden any time you like."

He walked slowly down the road, and William turned four cartwheels to celebrate the final wiping out of the insult. But the situation was a complicated one, and it seemed as if the meeting between the Colonel and Robert would complicate it still further. William, however, could not resist being present at this meeting, though he was poised on one foot, ready to turn and flee the minute the finger of guilt pointed in his direction.

Robert had spent the period of his retirement from the world brooding over the far from smooth course of true love, till the Colonel appeared to him to be a veritable monster of cruelty. It was a surprise, therefore, on emerging from the house for his first walk, well muffled and wearing the famous tweed coat, to find the Colonel waiting for him at the garden gate. His surprise increased when the Colonel seized his hand and said brokenly:

"Forgive me, my boy, forgive me."

Robert was deeply touched by the sudden repentance on the part of his enemy.

"It's quite all right, sir," he said. "Don't speak of it."

"I—I've done you a terrible wrong, my boy," went on the Colonel.

Robert, remembering the snubs he had suffered at the Colonel's hands, quite agreed with him, but was ready to be generous.

"That's quite all right, sir," he said again. "Please don't speak of it."

"I—I'm afraid I hurt you very much indeed," went on the Colonel.

"Well, sir, I can't say you didn't," said Robert, "but—but please don't speak of it."

"You're generous, my boy. Generous. Are you going down the road? Let me accompany you, my boy. Take my arm please."

Robert, rather bewildered by this sudden change of front, took the Colonel's arm, and, making the most of the wholly unexpected situation, said:

"What I've really been wanting to talk to you about,

sir, ever since I heard you were interested in it, is Roman Britain. The theory I incline to about the Roman remains at Cirencester . . ." And leapt breathlessly into one of the paragraphs he had learnt by heart from his book on Roman Britain.

The Colonel was enthralled. He completely forgot everything but the Roman remains at Cirencester. In fact, Robert soon began to regret having introduced them. Their possibilities as a subject of conversation seemed so unlimited. He had already repeated the two paragraphs he knew by heart. He had partially learnt a third but he wasn't really sure of it.

They had now reached Brent House, however, and the Colonel called Eleanor out to join them.

"She knows nothing," whispered the Colonel in a conspiratorial fashion as she came out, "don't speak of it to her."

"No, sir, I won't," said Robert, thinking that the Colonel was referring to the Roman remains at Cirencester, and, with rising spirits, discussed lighter subjects with her for the rest of the walk.

Mrs. Brown, who was at the gate watching for their return, asked the Colonel and Eleanor to come in to tea. The Colonel's deprecating manner rather bewildered her, but she was glad to see him being so very friendly (almost affectionate) with Robert, because she was so tired of hearing Robert tell William that he had ruined his life.

"I'm so glad to find this boy so much better," he said, placing a hand paternally upon Robert's shoulder.

"Yes, he's got over it very well," said Mrs. Brown.

"Better than I feared he would," said the Colonel.

This struck Mrs. Brown as rather an odd thing to

say, but, though a queer old man, he was evidently a kind one. Indeed his kindness to Robert was almost overpowering. Mrs. Brown put it down to his having been for a walk with him and so got to know him. Mrs. Brown held a touching belief that it was only necessary to know her children—even William—in order to love them.

William was listening with an amazed relief. He could hardly believe that Robert and the Colonel had actually come back from their walk with the misunderstanding still flourishing merrily between them. He had thought that at the first word one or other would have smelt a rat. He had not to wait long now, however. Already the Colonel was drawing in his breath as if for some momentous speech.

"Mrs. Brown," he said, "I think that the time has come to tell you something that only Robert and I know, and to offer you my heartfelt apologies."

Robert gaped at him. For one delirious moment he thought that the Colonel was going publicly to offer him Eleanor's hand. But the Colonel continued:

"What only Robert and I know, Mrs. Brown, is the cause of his recent severe illness."

"But I do know, Colonel," said Mrs. Brown.

"You do?" said the Colonel, much surprised.

"Yes, his tonsils are too big. I can't think why, because neither mine nor his father's are any size at all to speak of."

"No, Mrs. Brown," said the Colonel. "This noble boy has deceived you in order to shield me. His tonsils are not too big, or, if they are, it wasn't because his tonsils were too big that he crawled home in such a terrible state the other day. Or, if it was, they were enlarged as the result of a brutal attack by—by one old enough to know better. No, the truth is that on Monday afternoon, foolishly, perhaps, this boy snowballed me, and, very very foolishly, I knocked him down so violently that till I returned with help I thought I had killed him."

He looked round the table. Eleanor and Mrs. Brown were gazing at him with amazement, but their amazement was as nothing to the amazement of Robert. Only William was unmoved, his eyes fixed on the ceiling, his face wearing an expression of seraphic innocence.

"I—I—I—*snowballed* you?" gasped Robert.

"Yes, you young devil!" chuckled the Colonel, relieved to have got his confession off his chest, "and a jolly good shot you are, too. Soaked me to the skin. I can still feel the snow running down my back."

The angelic solemnity of William's face broke up for a second then quickly restored itself.

"I—I—I swear I never snowballed you, sir," gasped Robert faintly.

"Come, come, my boy," said the Colonel. "No need to keep that up any longer. Better let me make a clean breast of it. You never snowballed me? You'll be denying that I knocked you down next!"

"Yes, sir," said Robert still more faintly, "I certainly do."

Robert was pale and earnest. There was no mistaking his sincerity.

"Good heavens!" said the Colonel, "you mean to say you've no memory of it at all? I'm afraid there must have been concussion. I ought to have spoken up sooner. I think"—to Mrs. Brown—"that the doctor must be summoned again. To treat the boy for enlarged tonsils when he was suffering from concussion may be fatal."

But Mrs. Brown, who had been struck dumb with amazement, found her voice at last and assured the Colonel that Robert had been in bed on Monday afternoon. She had been in his bedroom all the time, so she could bear witness to it.

"WE MUST HAVE MANY OTHER TALKS," SAID THE COLONEL.
HE LEANT OVER AND SHOOK ROBERT BY THE HAND.

"But, great heavens!" gasped the Colonel. "I saw you as plainly as I see you now. A little pale perhaps, but quite recognisable. Apart from everything else I knew your coat. . . ."

He was assured yet again by both Mrs. Brown and Robert that it could not possibly have been Robert.

"Then it must have been a hallucination!" he said

in a voice of awe. "It can have been nothing else than a hallucination. I saw him with my own eyes as plainly as I see him now, dressed in his hat and coat.

". . . But," the Colonel turned to William, evidently remembering something else, "you said that he was unconscious."

"He was," said William innocently, "he was asleep. I thought that was what you meant."

"You said that his lawyer was with him."

"He was," said William, "his friend's a lawyer."

"You said that——" he tried to remember what else William had said, but failed to remember anything definite. "Well," he said kindly, "evidently our conversation was a series of misunderstandings, with, perhaps, a desire on your part, my boy, to pretend to understand remarks of mine that in the circumstances you couldn't possibly have understood. . . . No, it must have been a hallucination. A hallucination," he repeated, evidently growing reconciled to the phenomenon. "A hallucination sent me by Fate to show me the utter worthlessness of one in whom I had trusted, and to show me the worth and intellect of one whom I had ignorantly despised. I thoroughly enjoyed our talk on the Cirencester remains, my boy, and we must have many others."

He leant over and shook Robert warmly by the hand.

Robert grinned inanely, then turned to meet Eleanor's eyes. They were smiling at him fondly. They told him quite definitely that she really *had* liked him better than Archie all the time. He had to pinch himself to make sure that he was awake. It was all too wonderful to be true. And yet it was jolly mysterious. The old chap had said that he'd seen him as plainly as possible in his hat and coat. In his hat and coat . . . snowballing him. . . . He looked at William. William's face wore a shining look of innocence, his eyes were slightly upraised. Robert knew the look well. . . . That kid had been up to one of his tricks. That he knew something about all this. He'd get hold of that kid to-night, and he'd—— No, on second thoughts, Robert decided not to pursue any investigations that might alter the situation.

He was quite satisfied with the situation as it was.

THE END